The Ruthless

J Bree

Prologue

Atticus

Four Years Ago

"We can't keep meeting like this."

Luca pulls the cap down over his face a little more. "I know. This is important."

Crossing state lines is the only way we have any chance of keeping this meeting secret and secure. I left my property on one of my motorcycles, a performance machine that is faster than any of my vehicles. Covered entirely in leather and a full helmet, there's no way any of the Jackal's spies would have realized it's me.

I've been very quiet about this hobby of mine for a reason.

"As long as you're sure we weren't followed… what's the information? What could be this important that you'd risk almost a decade of work to meet me?"

He huffs and steps in closer to my body. "The Wolf is leaving the Bay."

It's not at all what I'm expecting from him.

Not even close.

"She can't. She's fourteen, how can she leave?"

He huffs under his breath at me. "Fifteen in a few weeks. She's going to apply for emancipation; she's gotten a scholarship."

I know exactly what he's going to say now before the words come out of his mouth. Sure, the Wolf leaving the Bay is news I need to know, but it's not worth the risk to deliver the news personally.

The Wolf attending Hannaford Preparatory Academy as a freshman with Avery and Ash Beaumont?

That I need to know.

"It's a move against me. The Jackal must have found out about her. Fuck, we're going to have to move on him now and to hell with the consequences."

Luca shakes his head and scratches the back of his neck. "No. He definitely hasn't, I've been over every inch of his plans with him and he doesn't know. Fuck, when she came and told him she was leaving? He didn't like that. After his falling out with the Butcher I think he's spiraling out of control and with the Wolf gone he's going to fucking lose it. Avery is safe for now, just as long as they don't… talk about you."

I keep my face locked down hard but we've been friends too long for him not to know just how worried this news has me. "There's no way Avery would ever look twice at a Mounty gutter rat. The Wolf won't hold her interest unless she walks in there and tells the whole school who she is."

I hesitate. The girl has always been quiet, reserved, and calculating in everything she does. If I hadn't seen her in action I wouldn't believe half the stories about her kills. She's unrivaled in the Bay, her skill set renowned and highly sought after.

If you want a blood-soaked massacre you call the Butcher.

If you want a knife in the dark, never seen or heard until your throat is already slit, you call the Wolf.

"I could offer to go with her? The Jackal will send men up there after her. I could be another set of eyes for you both and make sure they stay out of each other's way?"

It's tempting but he's too valuable to me where he is. "I'll send my own set of eyes. Good work bringing this to me; I'll take care of it."

Luca nods but he doesn't move away. I don't want to risk sticking around here for too long, the longer we stay the more we risk being caught, so I clap him on the shoulder and step away.

"There's something else."

I turn back to look at him and he hesitates before continuing, "The Butcher offered himself to her. The Wolf turned him down, but if things go south... he's going to come after us all for her death. Whatever calculations you run about this mess, factor that in."

He sounds like he's pleading for her life. "Are you to argue with me if I do decide she needs to go? Have you grown attached to the little orphan Mounty?"

He meets my eye without any remorse, speaking through his teeth at the rage that still fills him at the memory as he says, "Standing there and watching that psychopath smash her leg to pieces was the hardest fucking thing I've ever done. You know that."

I turn and walk away.

It wasn't the hardest thing I've ever done.

Leaving Avery in a school with the most infamous assassin in the Bay might be, but I don't plan on leaving the Wolf there for long.

I will do anything to keep Avery safe.

The Ruthless

Chapter One

No matter how hard I blink, the murder board I've stumbled upon stays the same.

I stare at it as if there's still some chance it will magically change and Atticus Crawford, the man I've spent the majority of my life in love with, hasn't been plotting out the deaths of my family, but there's no changing the facts of what's right before my eyes.

Ash is on that board.

Harley. Lips. Blaise. Every last person that I love more than anything is staring back at me. Aodhan makes sense to me, if anyone wanted my lover dead it would be Atticus. The rage he'd snarled at me in the storage room when he'd found out I wasn't a virgin had shown his hand a little more than he probably wanted to.

Ash is on the board.

There's a groan behind me again and I remember that there's a man chained and starving behind the glass there. Jesus

H. Christ, I need to get the hell out of here and find my head before I lose myself in the panic at once again having my entire world torn down around me by Atticus Crawford. The Crow of Mounts Bay, the rule follower, the man who built his entire empire by the book and who abhors the dark and dirty parts of the world he's taken control of.

Plotting out the death of the Wolf and her family is *not* by any goddamn book.

There's another groan, this one loud enough to startle me out of the processing haze I've gone into while trying to figure out exactly *what the fuck* is going on. I take some very quick, but very careful, photos of the murder board and what little of the man I can see with his back turned on me through the glass, and then I take to the stairs as quickly as I can.

They're just as steep and narrow on the way up as they were on the way down.

This was not how I planned on getting back into my cardio routine, but I'm still in impeccable shape, so I only really have to worry about watching my step and not falling down the severe incline. Breaking a leg or my freaking neck wouldn't do any of us any good.

Only Jackson has some kind of a clue about where I am, and I'm not sure he'd send help with all of the threats I've been sending his way. Illi would probably beat the truth out of him, but by the time he'd figured out that lead, I could be dead.

Or worse.

I might need to send the creepy asshole hacker a muffin basket or something just to be sure he'd send out the cavalry for me if this type of thing happens again.

It occurs to me that I might be panicking, just a little, but at least it's keeping my mind busy while I make it up the godforsaken steps and into the dark tunnel again.

I call Aodhan the *second* I have a signal on my phone.

I desperately want to call Ash, but even in my panic I know that it'll only make things worse, and this… *situation* cannot possibly handle anything worse.

Aodhan picks up, his voice drenched in worry without having any of the gory details yet. "Queenie? Why is the line so bad? Where the fuck are you?"

I take a deep breath and force my voice to stay calm and even. "Are you done with… whatever you needed to look into? I need a pickup. Now."

"What's happened? What the fuck has that asshole done this time?" Aodhan snarls, and I would get pissy at him for jumping to conclusions, but… I'm too busy trying not to peel my own skin off in disgust over the state of whoever the hell is chained up back down the stairs. Every time I blink, I can see the bones sticking out from under his skin.

"I need you to get Jack to pick me up. It's either that or I'm calling a cab and risking it. I… I found something. I found something, and I need to get out of here right *the hell* now."

I know I sound shrill and panicked, but I don't think Aodhan has ever really heard me like this before. He's heard a lot of different things come out of me but freaking the hell out over my entire life being a lie is not one of them.

"The same place he grabbed you earlier? Done, he's on his way now. Do you need me to come back, Queenie? Fuck it, I'm coming now."

I try to get my voice calm again. "No, no. I'm fine; I'm not in danger. Don't come and… don't call Lips yet. I'll call her once I'm out of here."

He grumbles under his breath, the calls of gulls behind him. "That's not fucking helping, Queenie; if you need to get out of there this bad then something has happened, and I'm not leaving you out there."

There's a sound down the tunnel and I pull the phone away from my ear as I try not to disgrace myself. I will my feet to be silent, because I can't stop walking, not even to avoid someone seeing me leave. This sort of frenzied escape gives me flashbacks to my childhood terror at the hands of Senior and for that alone I might never forgive Atticus.

When the sound stops and no one rushes down the tunnel to kill me, I put the phone back to my ear to find Aodhan freaking out.

"Avery fucking Beaumont, if you don't answer me soon I'm putting a Molotov cocktail through Crawford's fucking window, so help me God!"

"I'm fine; I thought I heard something. Please tell me Jack

is close?"

There's cursing and an argument down the line between Aodhan and Illi before finally, Aodhan mutters to me, "He's close, Queenie. He's breaking all of the fucking road laws to get to you. I'm finishing up here now, but we're over an hour away. Jack... Jack won't let anything happen to you."

I believe him, but that doesn't help the panic in me, desperately needing him here with me so I have *something* stable now that once again Atticus has turned everything upside down.

It kills me to hang up the phone but Illi's snarling is clear and I don't want to distract Aodhan from... whatever the hell they're actually doing. I mean, I know what they're doing because that tape of what happened in the Jackal's lair is out there somewhere, hanging over our heads like a freaking guillotine blade. But I don't know the details of who they're paying off or cutting to pieces... and honestly, I couldn't care less.

I just need it gone.

My phone buzzes again but instead of the reassurance from Aodhan that I'm expecting, I find a text message from Jackson.

Are you dead? I'm about to put in an Amber Alert for you with the Wolf.

An Amber Alert—even when he's supposedly concerned, the idiot is still making light of the situation.

I take a full minute to reply, the wording carefully chosen.

No need, I'm alive just like the man in Atticus' basement. You wouldn't happen to know who he has chained down there, do you?

His reply is much quicker.

Queenie, you know damn well I didn't even know there was a basement. How the fuck am I gonna know about Crawford's secret prisoners? I should've known he had a secret freak fetish hidden under all those fucking suits.

I still don't know for sure if I believe him; my trust isn't easy to win and Jackson has already broken it once before.

Another message comes through.

Should I start rifling through his fucking sock drawers and find out who it is? Whatever you need, I'm good for.

My gut reaction is that I don't want him to start looking into Atticus, but that is all about protecting the man I've spent more than half of my life chasing and obsessing over.

Ash was on that board.

Ash and Harley, Lips and Blaise—it doesn't matter how much I love Atticus, I could never blindly trust him and lead us all to our deaths. My mother did exactly that; she trusted Senior even when all the warning bells were screaming in her mind, because it was too damn scary to face the monster who had lied and stolen her heart.

I will never do the same.

Impress me, Coyote. Find the man in the basement and maybe I'll trust you again.

I'm not expecting him to take it seriously, especially since the Jackal is dead and his place as an ally isn't really in question outside of my family. No one knows about his little indiscretion of handing information over to the Devil without telling us about it.

Or the fact that Nate was very obviously related to Lips.

But his reply back to me actually… impresses me.

I'll have it to you by the time you wake up. There's nothing I can't find, and I'm not having the Wolf's Queenie underestimate me.

I wait inside the tunnel until Aodhan's text comes through saying Jack has arrived and I'm safe to walk out of the dark space. I would never admit it, but I was *this* close to calling Ash and making him wait on the line with me like some sort of security blanket. That would have been the stupidest idea possible but calling him when I'm worried or, frankly, terrified is my default. He's always the first person on my mind, followed very closely by Harley and Lips.

He'll always be the other half of my soul, the person I shared a womb with, and the brother who took on the world to keep me safe. Nothing will ever change that.

His photo was on that wall.

I think I could have handled it if it was only Lips' photo up there. It makes sense for Atticus to be looking into her, while he's not a member of the family she's still a threat on the board to him, but to find Ash there? Harley too?

I'm not sure there's an explanation that he could ever give me that would be able to explain this away. I'm not sure I can ever trust him again… those fragile foundations we'd built up after I found out he was the Crow smashed to pieces all over again.

I can't fucking do this.

I stumble a little over my own feet as I walk out of the tunnel opening at the edges of the trees, lucky that I'm wearing flat shoes for once in my life, and Jack lurches toward me with something close to horror in his eyes.

"Fuck, Avery, what the fuck happened to you? Are you hurt? Fuck, I need to call *mo rí*."

I have no clue who *Maury* is but I just want to get the hell out of here. "It's—I'm fine. Did Aodhan say... can I stay with you until he's back?"

I feel pathetic falling over my words like this, but I don't think I realized how shaken I was until I saw Jack.

He helps me into the car, buckling me in when my hands shake too much to do it myself. When he's back behind the wheel and weaving his way through traffic, he calls Aodhan through the car's Bluetooth.

"She's white as a fucking ghost and shaking like a leaf; where the hell am I taking her? Home?"

I can hear Illi's voice in the background, snarling at someone, but now that Jack is here, I've become too numb to really focus on it. It's as though the adrenaline has seeped out of me and now I'm a shaking shell of myself again.

How the hell has Lips lived like this all her life?

Aodhan covers the mouthpiece and answers something back, then says back down the line, "Take her back to my loft;

the Butcher has backup heading to the city now. Put her on the phone."

I need to keep myself together so they don't go charging into Atticus' fortress-like mansion before I can figure out what the hell is going on, so I swallow around the dryness in my mouth so my voice comes out without the panicked and breathy quality that I'd used before. "I'm here. Honestly, I'm fine to go home until you're back."

"No. No, whatever the fuck that asshole has done means he doesn't get to fucking know where you are. No one knows about the loft so you'll be safe there until I can get to you."

His voice clear and vibrating with rage, Illi calls out, "Listen to him, kid. Get your ass somewhere safe because I'm ready to fucking bleed half the city out after this goddamn night. Whatever that fuck, the Crow, has done has moved him from my shit-list to my to-kill list."

I swallow because those words should terrify me but… if that board really is his, and who else could it belong to, then I'll have to vote on whether he lives or dies.

If he's targeting Ash, he can't live.

I might not be able to live with myself for voting against him, but I also couldn't live knowing I'd saved his life for him to then kill my twin.

"I'll go to the loft. I'll stay there until we know what's going on with… everything."

Jack nods, his eyes still on the traffic in front of us, and

Aodhan murmurs something reassuring down the line again. "Call the Wolf. Stay on the line with her while you wait for me; she's been pissed and ready for an update for hours."

I agree and Jack hangs up. My fingers are numb where they're curled so tightly around my own phone, barely registering it buzzing in my hand with messages from my family. They have no idea what's happened, only that Aodhan has had to remove me from Atticus' care once again and they're out for his blood.

Thank God they're thousands of miles away in Texas dealing with bikers, blood and death.

"Did he hurt you?" Jack murmurs again, his eyes sliding off of the road to look me over again. I shake my head and he frowns at me, clearly thinking I'm lying.

"I didn't see him. I didn't see anyone, I just... found something. I wasn't safe there, especially if he found out that I'd seen it." My voice is too soft, too *fucking* fragile once again, but he finally looks as though he believes me.

We make it through the busy downtown and past all of the seedy bars that Lips spent her teenage years working her jobs in, collecting information and doing hits on unsuspecting criminals. I know nothing about what it means to frequent those places, but I know everything about what it takes to be the Wolf. Every scenario that Lips has ever run me through flicks through my head as if on a movie reel, the ways she was cornered and fought back, all of the times she took down men three times her size with nothing but her knife and an uncanny ability to read the situations she was in.

I'm constantly in awe of her.

"The loft is secure and private. Barely anyone knows it exists and only *mo rí* and I know he's the one who owns it. I'll stay with you."

I nod and try to smile at him, but it's stiff at best. We're only a block away from Illi's warehouse apartment when he turns into an old grocery store parking lot, parking the car in the darkest corner possible. It's filthy and not at all what I was expecting, with a few cars parked closer to the store's doors. It's a twenty-four hour place, the type you expect to get shot in for a dollar, and I'm instantly uneasy.

"There is absolutely no way on this Earth that I'm going in there," I say, my tone exactly that of a spoiled rich brat.

It makes complete sense.

"Relax, Queenie. This is just the hiding place for the entrance. Nobody comes here, no one except some old gang members marked by the Ox and working girls who're desperately flirting with death. No one would ever guess the loft was here too."

I grimace and nod because he's correct, I would never guess that Aodhan would willingly sleep near this place. Jack gets out of the car and walks around to get my door, giving me an arm to hold like a gentleman. I almost stumble on my feet because I've forgotten that I'm wearing flat shoes, my outfit completely out of my usual attire.

No wonder Jack was so worried.

"It's through here; we should move quickly so we're not seen," Jack murmurs quietly even though there's no one around us, and I let him lead me past the grocery store building and down the alley to an old fire escape.

Never had I ever thought I'd be climbing one of these but tonight has been a nightmare so why the hell not?

Jack ushers me up first, following closely behind and promising he'll catch me if I slip and fall. It's sweet and everything, but I hadn't even considered that I might slip and now my knees are shaking like a freaking leaf.

When I finally get to the top, there isn't a door waiting for me at all, only a small platform to stand on and a window that is barred with a blackout curtain on the inside so I can't see a thing. When Jack heaves himself onto the tiny platform with me, I start to panic a little that maybe he's not such a good guy and he's going to throw me off of the side of the building.

He grins at me and pulls a key out, sliding into a hole I hadn't noticed in my freakout, and the window swings open like a mini door.

"After you, Queenie. Your tower awaits."

The Ruthless

Chapter Two

The loft is… something out of a dream.

Nothing in it is to my specific taste, I can't imagine ever picking anything in here out for myself, but it's all absolutely freaking perfect. The floors are all old wood, worn and warm, the kind of beauty that can't be bought new but has to be broken in over decades.

There's a new rug in dark greens and grays in the kitchen area, and the cupboards are a rich oak with a simple stone counter top. All of the appliances are brand new, though none of them are the top of the line which makes sense to me.

There's a giant mirror with a beautiful gold leaf frame leaning against one of the walls, almost reaching the ceiling, and facing it is a mattress on the floor covered in pillows and blankets until it looks like a plush nest I want to climb into and never get out of.

There's no TV, no computer, no front door, nothing of the outside world in here to disturb me. It takes me a second to find the bathroom door, slightly ajar and a claw-foot bathtub peeking out.

It's perfect and everything I didn't know that I so desperately need right now.

"There's food in the fridge and everything is clean in here; *mo rí* said you'd be worried about that. Go eat and shower and… fucking relax. Whatever. He'll be home soon. I'm going to go move the car so no one sees it and recognizes it. They'd never find this place but better safe than sorry. You gonna be okay to just wait here?"

I nod, stooping down to slide my shoes off because I hate shoes in living areas like this, and he heads off, the clunking noise of the bolt in the window sliding into place a soothing thing.

I'm safe.

I'm alone.

I can breathe.

Why the hell didn't Aodhan bring me here in the first place? I might be alone here, but the loft's location is so obscure that I don't need security climbing all over me. This is the perfect safe house in the city.

I leave my shoes by the window and walk around the room a little more, poking and prodding at the very minimal decor in here. There's a bowl on the breakfast bar with some keys and loose change in it, a ticket stub from a movie I've never even heard of in there. There's a Chinese menu in one of the drawers from a restaurant a few blocks away. The kitchenware is very basic but enough that I can cook dinner and very basic desserts. The fridge is well stocked; the milk is well within its expiration so Aodhan's been here recently.

The bathroom is immaculate.

Top notch, perfectly clean and the products under the sink are all the same types and brands that I use. That's soothing to me somehow, because that's how deranged the clean freak in me really is, and there's soaps hidden under the sink that he definitely picked out with me in mind.

I don't care that I sound conceited, there's no denying the scents he picked are for me.

I take one of them and run the bath as hot as I can possibly stand without screaming. He's not here to frown and grunt at me over how I clean myself, so the first bath is brutal as I scour the horrors of the night away.

When my skin is aching and raw, I let the water out and run a second bath at a more tolerable temperature.

I almost fall asleep in it.

By the time the sun is rising, I'm tucked up in one of Aodhan's shirts and a pair of sweatpants that I have to roll the waist up six times to make them work, a coffee in my hands as I sit on the mattress and just... freak the hell out about what I'm going to do because this is do or die time.

If I choose the wrong thing, a lot of people could die.

I'm swallowing the last mouthful of my now tepid coffee when my phone rings again, Lips' ringtone, and I can't keep ignoring my family without them charging back home to rescue me.

"Am I killing him?"

No hi, how's things—typical Mounty. "Which him are we talking about? Because my kill list is at least seventy percent male."

She scoffs down the line at me. "Of course it is, men are perverts and fucking creeps. I'm actually surprised it's not higher."

I giggle at her and put the cup down on the ground, sinking back against the pillows. "I'm not sure if we're killing him, Lips."

The line goes dead quiet.

I don't know where she's managed to sneak off to that it's so quiet, but I don't even hear her breathing. I'm about to check she's still there when she speaks again, her voice entirely the fabled Wolf of Mounts Bay.

"What the fuck did he do to you?"

I almost fucking cry. "Nothing. He didn't do a goddamned thing. He left when I got home and I… decided to poke around a bit. I found a set of stairs to the basement, and I found something there."

I pause for a second, trying to figure out exactly how much of this I'm going to tell her, but she doesn't say a word. She just waits me out because she trusts me just as much as I trust her.

I adore her.

I fumble a little but I choke the truth out. "There's someone locked in his basement, Lips. There's an emaciated, disgusting man down there who looks as though he's living in his own filth and going without regular meals… and that's not even the worst part. He has a murder board there too. You're on it. The… our whole family is on it."

Silence.

"Ash is on the board, Lips. With his eyes crossed out."

Still nothing.

I start to panic a little bit, mostly because I'm sure that she's slipped fully into a rage blackout and innocent roadies and tech support guys might *die* if they walk in on her right now. Not that I couldn't fix it for her, but then the guys would all get involved.

I don't want Ash anywhere near Mounts Bay right now for so many freaking reasons.

"Are you one hundred percent sure it's a murder board?" she says, her voice dark and dripping with rage.

I stop for a second.

What the hell else could it have been?

"It was a lot of photos on the wall, most of us with our eyes crossed out… the way the Collector has been leaving me photos."

Lips hums under her breath. "Did you take photos? Who else is on there? I want to fucking gut Atticus for this but, I've got to be honest, I don't see him wanting to kill Ash. Take a swing at him every time he opens his mouth? Sure. Kill him and hurt you? No. I just don't."

I let out my breath and switch her to speakerphone, sending the photos through and then looking through them myself. There's dozens of people I don't know up there, plus the entire Crawford family. Amanda Donnelley isn't up there, which I don't know if it's a good thing.

When I say this to Lips, she hums again. "Maybe she's the psycho sending the fucking photos? Maybe this is him collecting evidence and the creepy fucking 'warning' photos. Why the fuck he'd be hiding them in a basement, I don't know, but that shit still makes more sense to me than him planning Ash's murder."

A desperate sounding laugh rips out of me. "What about you? Do you think he'd kill you? And Harley and Blaise?"

She doesn't hesitate. "I think he's had a target painted on me from the moment I won the scholarship to Hannaford. I think Harley could've gone either way, depending on how he treated you… and I think Atticus, no matter what he says otherwise, would've paid me a black diamond and a favor to take Blaise out if you'd fallen for him. Aves, you need to watch Aodhan's back, because Atticus is only a rule enforcer when the rules work in his favor. He'd break them all for you."

That's… not at all what I was expecting from her.

Atticus has pushed me away at every chance, pushed me into Aodhan's arms really because my heart was broken and bleeding all over the freaking place when I found him, so to think of him actually wanting me, wanting me enough to risk his position and his standing in the Twelve to get to keep me, it's unfavorable to me.

I became the Crow for you.

"I'll keep Ash out of Mounts Bay until you know what is really going on. No one will ever get close to him, I swear to you."

I know for sure she's telling the truth.

No one touches the Wolf.

It's almost lunchtime when Aodhan finally arrives at the loft, his clothes ripped up and covered in blood and dirt.

I'm standing in the kitchen, waiting for the brownies to finish off in the oven, and his eyes are a little desperate as they dart around the open space before they finally land on me, softening immediately.

"There's my girl, fuck, I thought you'd climbed out the bathroom window for a second there."

I huff at him and prop a fist onto my hip, ridiculous looking with the oven gloves on I'm sure. "And why the hell would I do that, O'Cronin?"

He smirks at me, all Irish charm that definitely doesn't turn my insides to mush, and toes off his shoes at the window to leave them with mine. "You're becoming a seasoned escape artist; I think I'll always be chasing after you at this rate."

I shrug at him as he stalks into the bathroom, shedding his clothes on the way but holding onto them to throw them all in the washing basket in there. There's no laundry in the loft that I've been able to find, so I guess he takes it all with him when he goes back to the O'Cronin compound.

He showers while I finish up with the desserts, waiting until the pan of brownies cools enough to dish us each up a bowl with huge scoops of ice cream. I have no idea if he'll even enjoy the sugar explosion after his day, but Lips never said no to my panicked dessert baking and I need the sugar right now like I need air.

I do the cardinal sin and I sit in the bed to eat it.

I never, ever, eat in bed.

Ever.

But there's something about this loft that makes me... different. I know it can't actually change me as a person, I still eat so freaking carefully so I don't spill anything, but it's as though I can be the most calm and relaxed version of myself here.

The best Avery Beaumont I can be... without the manic, deranged psycho destroying everything with a scrubbing brush. Well, today anyway. Maybe after a good nine hours of sleep, I'll be back to my wicked ways.

Aodhan gets out of the bathroom in nothing but a towel, raising his eyebrows at the bowl waiting for him on the counter, but he takes it without a word. The stag tattoo on his chest is magnificent, my eyes drawn to it, and the way it moves with his chest is captivating. If my mind wasn't busy running through my conversation with Lips, over and over again, I might just be fantasizing about running my tongue over the edges of it until the shape was burned into my mind for the rest of time.

"If you're cooking up sweets then we're all in trouble, not that I didn't already know," he says as he lowers himself down onto the mattress, groaning a little.

The edge of the towel splits a little and shows me his entire leg right up to those sculpted thighs of his. I don't want to move my eyes away from them, but there's too much information hanging in the air around us.

Instead of saying a word, I get my phone out and I hand it to him with the photos showing.

I'd thought a lot about what I would say to him about this, whether I should lie about it or withhold the details until Lips and I had figured out a little more about what the hell is going on.

But I don't lie to Aodhan.

Not about Atticus, not when he's been far too understanding about the entire situation and always respected not only my feelings but my decisions when it comes to the other man who holds my heart.

"Fuck. Fucking Christ, was this in his house? Is he the one threatening you? Trying to drive you into his arms or some shit? Fuck, even Jack is up there."

Jack and Aodhan and a handful of other O'Cronins I've never met before, but Lips had listed them all off to me to make note of. There were only four people she couldn't name in the photos, but she's going to send them through to Illi because she's sure he'd know.

I'll ask Aodhan too. "It was in his secret basement. Unlisted in the house plans, the Coyote didn't even know it existed. Lips— Lips and I are still trying to figure out his motives; we have a few leads. I'm sorry I freaked out. Seeing Ash up there… broke me."

Aodhan nods and flicks through the photos again, the spoon hanging out of his mouth. "Our night was just as bad. I think I've seen every inch of the human body from the inside today. Illi is too fucking good at carving people up, and he hasn't taken the photos being out lightly. He— fuck, Queenie, he loves you the way a big brother does. He might even be more fucking fierce than Ash."

I smile at him with the tiniest of shakes of my head. "You haven't seen my brother in full Beaumont mode. Don't get me wrong, Illi is definitely the Butcher and he lives up to all of the horror stories but Ash… Ash is everything our father ever wanted in a son, except he only uses that brutal rage to protect me and Lips. Or Harley and Blaise, but they've rarely needed it. I would never, ever, bet against Ash and that has nothing to do with my loyalty to him."

Aodhan nods slowly and takes another bite. "Your dad was a serial killer, right? Harley said some fucked-up shit about him, and I thought he was just trying to scare me off of you."

I giggle at him, placing my empty bowl on the floor next to the mattress before lying down. "From the time I started counting, Joseph Beaumont Sr. had over four hundred victims. All of them killed to fulfill his sexual deviancy and need for complete sadistic control."

There's something reassuring about the way Aodhan suddenly looks sick. I need a man who can kill without question but I also need that man to have a soul and a moral line. I get that we're not pious, noble people, but I do draw the line at raping and killing innocent women and girls. Christ, some of Senior's victims were teenage girls stolen in other countries and sent to America to be sold at auction.

Just like Odie was.

I feel that same disgust and rage at the thought of it.

Aodhan puts his bowl down as well and rolls to face me. "The Wolf killed him?"

I nod. "She walked into our childhood home with a gut full of stitches and almost died to protect Ash and I. I've never been so terrified in my whole life. She just—she left in the middle of the night and by the time we realized, there was no making it in time."

He nods slowly, his eyes dropping down to the necklace he'd returned to me with his diamond and the Wolf's diamond resting there between my breasts. "Everything she did for you all, all of the moves and risks she made, she's one in a fucking million. No wonder she snared three grown men to an obsession."

I laugh too loud at that, but the awed tones in him are adorable. It's exactly the way I feel about her too, awed and obsessed and so freaking grateful to call her my best friend. My sister.

He smirks at me and leans forward to grab my chin, pressing our lips together in a light kiss that ends far too quickly. When he pulls away, I have to force myself not to chase his lips because I don't want to look as desperate as I really am for him. I need his stability, the way he says what he means and is always true to his word. I need the firm and sure way that he takes me apart and owns my body, the way that he's focused on nothing but me and the pleasure between us.

I need the way that he loves me, even if neither of us are ready to say it yet.

His voice is rough as he says, "Illi has his bikers out patrolling. They're a little less... mouthy about you these days. I think he might've thrown down about you. We're safe to just... be here today, without worrying about who's gonna find us."

I nod. "I trust you and I trust Illi to keep us safe. Now I need you to fuck me until I can't think or move or exist. I need to forget about evil plots and murder boards and fucking sex tapes. Please, Aodhan."

His eyes flare wide and a little snarl leaves his throat. "You don't even have to ask me for that, Queenie, and you don't ever have to say fucking please."

The Ruthless

Chapter Three

It doesn't matter that my eyes are starting to sting with exhaustion and my mind is still an absolute mess thanks to Atticus and the games he's caught up in, the moment Aodhan pulls me back into his lips, my body melts for him.

There's been too much going on, too many things getting between us, and the stroke of his tongue against mine is like a sedative. Nothing else matters but the way I fit against his body and the feel of his hands cupping my face.

Everything about his movements are a slow torture. There's nothing frenzied or rushed about the way that he's slowly pulling me apart, piece by piece.

I get impatient.

I want to forget about everything happening outside of this little safe haven he's created; I want to only exist for the two of us and the pleasure we can find in each other, but there's no rushing him.

The moment I try, he pulls back. "If you want mind-numbing, leg-shaking, brain-breaking sex then quit trying to speed things up. You need to learn the difference between a quick fuck and me spreading you out and making a meal of you."

My thighs clench together a little at the sound of that, and a slow smirk cuts across his face. He's too attractive right now, too open and present and right here with me in this vulnerable moment.

I want to squirm away but he won't let me, the grip of his hands on my face gentle but unyielding. I have no choice but to hold his eyes with my own and watch as he slowly tips my head back and kisses his way down my throat. The scratch of his stubble against the soft skin of my neck is like the perfect torture, rough enough to have me gasping even as he licks and sucks the sting away. There isn't going to be an inch of my skin unmarked by the time he's through with me.

He continues his slow torture until he reaches the opening of the shirt I'm wearing, his unhappy groaning at my skin being covered the only warning he gives me before he reaches up to yank it over my head.

I wish he'd hurry up and push inside me, something, anything, because I feel so fucking empty without his body covering mine and filling me, pushing and pushing until I want to burst.

I never want this to end.

His tongue circles one of my nipples before his teeth clamp

down hard enough that a moan rips out of my throat and my hands tangle in his hair. When he moves to give that same treatment to my other nipple, my hands make a fist and tug until he's grunting and grinding his hips against mine mindlessly.

I feel like a teenager.

I mean, I'm barely twenty years old but I never really went through the mindless makeout and grinding stage. Not really. Rory was the closest I came and that relationship was over before it started.

When Aodhan has kissed and scraped and sucked his way down to my hips, he shoves the sweatpants away and presses a kiss to the wet heat between my legs, my pussy already dripping from his slow seduction. I don't think it would take much for me to come right now, one finger hooking inside me or the brush of the heel of his palm against my clit, anything would set me off.

Then he pulls away.

I don't rise to the bait because I'm sure this is just the next level of teasing he has planned for me but then he tugs the towel off of his waist and throws it away and for a split second I think that he's going to fuck me into next week, just what I need.

He lowers himself down… onto the bed next to me, splaying himself out like this is all done and over with.

I'm about to bitch him out into next week when he chuckles at me, his hand grabbing my wrist and tugging me over to him. "Climb up, Queenie. Get that pretty pussy on my face."

There's a lot of things about sex that I'd always found

distasteful. To crawl over someone, naked, and have myself splayed open over their face? No thank you, that sounds like a horror story.

I'm just desperate enough to give it a go.

Except that Aodhan groans like a dying man the moment I straddle his face, his chest heaving and his hands more desperate now on my skin than they've been since he got home, and if that doesn't make my confidence skyrocket then nothing will. His fingers spread me open, adjusting my legs until he's practically smothering himself with my pussy, and I almost cry when his lips finally touch my clit.

I try to ease up a little, just shift away so he can breathe, but he lets out a snarl that sends vibrations straight to my clit until my legs shake.

I have to take a deep, calming breath before I can focus on anything other than what his mouth is doing to me. I don't want to be a pillow princess and just lie back while he does all of the work.

I want to make him feel just as good as he makes me feel.

With only two blowjobs under my belt, it's a little intimidating to be in this position. Add that to how I'm attempting to make this a mind meltingly good blowjob and the pressure is on.

The French manicure on my fingernails looks strangely obscene wrapped around his dick and I wish he could see it but then his tongue flicks against my clit again and I'm gasping and trying to remember to stay on task.

Suck his brains out of his dick, Beaumont, for Christ's sake!

I dive into the blowjob the same way I tackle anything, head first and with the false confidence of someone who has always gotten what they wanted, one way or another.

I relax my throat enough to swallow him down in one go and the groan he lets out is that of a dying man, long and choked out as though he's in pain. It gives me the confidence to not only keep going but to put my all into it, no matter how I look or the sounds I'm making.

Humming works quite well and almost backfires on me because the groan he lets out over my clit takes me all the way to the edge in one go, the wave of my orgasm washing over me until my legs are shaking and just barely keeping me up.

The embarrassment of falling on him might kill me.

I desperately want him to come first, even if that does put a dampener on the rest of my plans, but no matter what noises he makes in appreciation of what I'm doing, he doesn't want to lose this game we've found ourselves in. He also knows exactly how to shove me over the edge and when I reach down to cup his balls gently, rolling him in my hand, he obviously gets close enough to coming that he finally stops his teasing and gets to work properly, two fingers slipping inside of me and hooking until he's stroking over my G spot mercilessly.

I almost choke, I come so hard with him so far down my throat it hurts.

I forget sometimes how strong he is when all of my limbs

start to shake and I think I'm about to fall, his hands wrap around my hips and lift me off of him, maneuvering my body until I'm straddling his waist now and not his face.

"There's no way I'm riding anything right now, give a girl a break," I say, hoping my voice doesn't sound as wrecked as I'm feeling.

He grins up at me, his face drenched and glistening with my cum that he's made no attempts to wipe away. "You look too fucking pretty sitting on me; let a man enjoy the view for a minute."

I blush like a schoolgirl and my eyes narrow at him for making me so goddamn soft, but his grin just gets bigger and more lecherous.

I'm not expecting him to flip me over, his hand cradling the back of my head so the impact onto the pillows doesn't jar me and by the time I've realized what it is that he's doing, he's finally, *finally*, pushing inside of me.

There's nothing like this feeling. Nothing at all in the world compares to Aodhan O'Cronin sliding inside of me like he's coming home, and he doesn't at all ease me into it. His hips move rhythmically, not pounding into me but relentless as he stokes my body into a frenzy.

I'm a squirming mess but one of his hands clamps onto my chin and holds my face steady as he stares down at me, taking in every shaking moan and desperate gasp until I'm coming, my pussy clenching around him and his hips stuttering for a second as he groans.

He doesn't come though.

The control he's got over himself right now is fucking unreal, and the moment I come down from my high, his hips start up again. It's not until my body is breaking apart for the fourth time that he grunts and grinds his hips into mine, his lips desperate on mine as we both groan through the high.

My legs are numb so he definitely did exactly what he said he was going to do.

He leans down to press his forehead against mine, his breath fanning out across my cheeks before he pulls out and away from me, and it's a more intimate moment than when I'd straddled his smirking face.

I think I'm in love with him.

It shouldn't shock me at all, I wouldn't let him in if I didn't think that this could be something serious, but I didn't think I was close to those feelings yet.

It almost feels like it's rushed... because my feelings for Atticus have been with me forever and to find someone else so quickly and to fall so hard feels freaking terrifying.

And just like that, my brain clicks back on and there's no escaping from everything swirling around in there, processing and assessing and calculating the risks and rewards.

I want nothing more than to curl up in Aodhan's arms and sleep for the next month. It's so unlike me, I never run from the hard stuff like this and I'm always planning out our next moves, but right now that seems... terrifying.

What if our next moves are to kill Atticus?

"Stop thinking about it, Queenie. Stop worrying about what the asshole is doing, that's tomorrow's problem. Fuck, maybe we need to go again to ram that home for you."

I roll my eyes at the suggestive tones, but a smile creeps over my face. Nobody is perfect, no matter how much they mean to me, but Aodhan comes pretty close.

I used to think the same of Atticus.

Jesus H. Christ, I'm never going to be able to get him out of my head.

"This is the way my brain works; I can't shut it off. Get some sleep, you've been up for longer than I have."

He lets out a breath and shuts his eyes, the exhaustion still radiating off of him in waves. He looks like the last two days have aged him, like the grinning and easygoing guy that has become such an important part of my life has been replaced with a world-weary man.

Okay, that might be a little dramatic of me to say but of the two men who have found their way into my heart, he's the balance. He's the one who manages to walk that line between treating me like I know what the hell I'm doing and trying to make me enjoy life just a little more. He doesn't coddle me or protect me into captivity.

He wants me to live.

I lean over to kiss him softly and then I pull away to grab

my phone from where it's fallen the short distance to the floor. There's a dozen messages from Ash, all of them worried and savage in his hatred of Atticus. I know Lips wouldn't have told him any of the details, but my brother hates Atticus enough that he doesn't need details.

He only needs to hear his name.

Lips has sent through some more theories and the names of the photos she didn't recognize thanks to Illi. Everything is vague in that way that she is in messages, too worried about being hacked and having her messages land in the wrong hands.

It's a valid concern.

You can ruin someone's whole life with a handful of screenshots.

There's also a message from Jackson to call him when I wake up which has me wincing at the idea that I still haven't gone to sleep yet. I move to get out of the bed so I don't disturb Aodhan, though there's only the bathroom to hide in, but his arm snakes around me and holds onto me tight.

"I need to make a call. Just get some sleep and I'll be back in a minute."

He grunts and pulls me in closer. "You're not fucking leaving this bed. Call people, threaten them, plan a coup—I don't give a fuck, but your ass isn't moving."

I huff at him like I'm annoyed but he's a little too charming for me right now because I need to focus on my work for a minute.

I dial Jackson's number and he picks up almost instantly. "Good morning, my liege."

Christ. "What have you found, Jackson; I'm not in the mood for games."

He grunts at me and I hear the sounds of his fingers on the keyboard. He has one of those loud, extra clicky types that would make me want to murder him if I were Viola.

Thank God I'm not.

Being stuck with Jackson in the bunker is a fate worse than hell.

"Did you recognize the guy in the basement at all? Was there, like, anything at all about him that seemed familiar to you?"

I roll my eyes and huff at the idiot. "If I did recognize him, why the hell would I ask you to figure out who he is? Honestly, Jackson—"

"There's no security cameras in the tunnel or the basement, obviously, because I didn't even know the basement existed. So I had to go through the security footage to figure out who went into the house and has never come out."

I shrug, that's obvious enough. "How far back did you go?"

He groans. "I went as far back as it took for someone not to fucking leave the place. Crawford doesn't shit where he eats, thank God, so it's not like I had to look for body bags either."

Aodhan pulls me further into his body, tucking me in close and burying his face into my neck while he tries to sleep through the phone call.

Just once I'd like to enjoy it rather than dealing with this bullshit.

"The only person who has gone in but not out was his brother, Bingley. The Butcher delivered him there four years ago and the pervert has never left."

Bingley.

Jesus H. Christ, could it have been him? I didn't get a good look at the guy, the smells and moaning were terrifying and I was too goddamn distracted by the murder board to get a proper photo of him, but... I mean, it could have been. Four years of captivity and if Atticus wasn't exactly taking care of him then it definitely could have been him.

Why the hell would he be keeping him down there?

The obvious answer is that Bing is a pedophile who was possibly worse than Randy and Holden in his depravity because he aimed his perversions at innocent children, but why not just kill him? If Atticus paid the Butcher to find him and bring him in then why not just get him taken care of in a more permanent way?

Obviously, Randy and Holden don't know that Atticus has him locked up, so he could have easily hidden his death. Illi has access to cannibals, for Christ's sake, they don't exactly leave much evidence behind!

I'm going to have to speak with him.

I don't want to but there's too many inconsistencies, too

many variables, too many different scenarios that could be happening. He could be innocent.

As innocent as the Crow can be.

"Thank you, Jackson. As always your work is impeccable."

He huffs down the line at me. "Does this mean I'm off your shit list? I like breathing."

I hum at him, the same way Lips does when she's toying with people's lives in her head and I swear I can hear him start to sweat. "You're awfully worried about what I think of you these days. Where has the snarky, sarcastic hacker asshole gone that we all know and tolerate?"

He's quiet for a second, only the beeping and whirring sounds of his computer to be heard. "I've got Viola to think about. She's only got me now that her family disowned her, and I've done a fuckload of bad shit in my time that might bite us in the ass. I can't have you sending the fucking Devil here to take me out."

Aodhan doesn't react at all, his breathing still even, so he's either asleep or didn't hear him. "I thought your bunker was bomb-proof? You've never worried about someone showing up before."

He lets out a shaky breath. "The Devil got in. Fuck knows how he did it, but he got in here the day he came calling about the Wolf. I haven't slept right since."

The Ruthless

Chapter Four

When I finally fall asleep after a brief visit to the bathroom for a cleanup, I sleep right through until long after dark. My body clock is all out of order and I feel sick the moment my eyes open, groaning and searching in the bed for my phone.

I find Aodhan instead.

He's awake, sitting up and on his phone, something I very rarely see him do with me around. The moment my hand touches him he glances over at me with a lazy smirk before leaning down and kissing me softly.

"Good evening, sleeping beauty."

I frown at him, completely aware that I look like a mess in the mornings even when I can do my usual nightly routine, so I must be freaking hideous. "What's the time? Why are you looking so… alive? I feel like death."

He chuckles under his breath and strokes back my hair, far too sweet for me this early. Or late, I guess. "It's almost midnight, Queenie. You were fucking *out* like a light. I had to switch your phone to silent because it's been going crazy."

When my eyes narrow at him, he holds up a hand. "I told Lips, Harley and Illi you were sleeping, so if it was an emergency, they'd have called me. Everyone else can fucking wait."

It's flawed logic but, again, sweet of him.

I go for another shower to wash the sleep and sex away. Who would've ever thought that I, Avery 'germaphobe' Beaumont, would be able to fall asleep after sex with only a quick cleanup and not a complete shower? It must be like that dick magic Lips always finds herself caught in when those idiot boys drag her into public sex acts even though she knows better.

I miss her.

I shower and wash out my mess of hair, the curls no longer sexy waves and now firmly in the bird's nest territory. I take my time to scrub down, shave my legs, and exfoliate until my skin is baby soft and perfectly pink for the mild abuse.

When I walk back out in a towel, Aodhan is cooking us both breakfast, his boxer shorts hanging a little low on his hips. He's cleaning as he goes, brownie points there, and the plates are a muted gray, also acceptable.

"Grab another one of my shirts; we can go find some clothes for you in the morning."

I scoff but wander back over to the bedroom area, stepping carefully around the mattress to the rustic drawers. It takes a minute to dig around until I can find something that will only look ridiculous on me and not completely fucking stupid. As I pull the fabric over my head, I take in a lungful of the laundry detergent he uses and the faint scent of him still clinging to the fabric.

Huh.

I wasn't expecting to like that but there's something... soothing about it. I can't explain it and I wouldn't want to try. Except maybe to Lips, who would fundamentally understand, because I'm almost positive that she's completely switched out her closet with clothes she's stolen from her little harem of obsessed, idiot boys.

I find a pair of shorts with a drawstring and pull them on as well, no interest in walking around with a bare ass, and then I take a seat at the breakfast bar. Aodhan slides a plate over to me, the fluffy looking omelette spilling over the sides, before taking a seat next to me.

It's delicious, but I'd murder for a coffee.

"No caffeine. You'll feel like shit drinking it this late."

I huff at him. "What are you, a mind reader now? Also, you're underestimating me. There is never a bad time for coffee."

He chuckles at me, shaking his head. "I spent a lot of years living on all sorts of time schedules thanks to the fishing docks and trying not to drop outta school. Trust me, don't drink the coffee until the sun comes up."

It still sounds like blasphemy but I work my way through my food. It isn't just cooked to perfection, he seasoned it well and precooked the bacon. Even Harley's eggs aren't this good and that boy is excellent at breakfast foods.

His French toast is incredible too.

I do the last of the dishes when we're both finished, feeling too wired to slip into the casual and relaxed state Aodhan seems to be in. I understand that this is his little safe house, his getaway from the stresses of his life as the head of the O'Cronin family and the newest member of the Twelve, but I plan murder plots in my downtime. I read thousands of pages of police reports and blackmail hotel staff for extortion material.

I can't just sit around and wait for daylight.

Aodhan gets a phone call and locks himself in the bathroom to take it. It's clearly about the next job his cousins are doing down at the loading docks so I'm not at all interested in eavesdropping. Instead I set myself back up on the bed, because there's nowhere else to sit comfortably, and go through all of the messages I've missed.

Blaise has sent me a video of Lips singing karaoke with him in some disgusting dive bar at one of their stops. It starts with her looking like she's going to puke all over him, but by the end she's relaxed and giving it her all. She's freaking incredible and in the corner of the shot I can see Ash staring at her like she's the center of his world, like the sun rises and falls each day at her command and he has no choice but to worship her.

I take a screenshot of it and send it to Lips.

The way he loves her is the type of love that lasts forever and nothing would make me happier than knowing they'll grow old together.

The other two as well, obviously, but Ash had always been so harsh and disinterested in girls… I didn't think he'd ever fall for someone.

"Who was that singing? Another band on tour with your family?" Aodhan says, the bed dipping as he lounges down next to me.

"No, that's the Wolf of Mounts Bay's secret talent. One she guards well because of what the Jackal did to her. We're all obsessed with her voice; Morrison put her on his album because he wanted to listen to her on repeat for the rest of his life."

His eyebrows hit his hairline and I giggle, turning the phone so he can watch the video too. "They all really do love her. I can see why she didn't want to choose."

I nod, swallowing because we can't talk about choosing without the other man in our relationship looming over us. "The four of them are so goddamn codependent that they would've never worked out with monogamy. Ash would have pined for her for the rest of his life; he's a forever sort of person."

Aodhan nods and kisses my shoulder. "You are too. How long have you waited for Crawford? You're still agonizing over these photos because of the consequences he might be facing from your family."

There's nothing really I can say back because he's exactly right.

Illi texts me back to confirm he had taken Bingley to the

Crow's fortress some years ago, he also tells me where he found the pervert so the food in my gut starts roiling.

Aodhan reads it over my shoulder, grunting in disgust. "That's another mark in his favor... keeping *that* off of the street."

I hum under my breath. "Why not just kill him? It would have to be easier to just dispose of him rather than feeding him and... well, letting him exist for all of this time?"

Aodhan grunts and shrugs. "Fuck knows what's going through his head. Every man, woman, and child in the Bay knows that the Crow is at the center of a giant web of secrets, lies, and classified intel. Bing obviously knows something, or is worth something to someone. Would their parents pay out for him? What do they think of their pedophile son?"

They think far too highly of him, like his tastes are a quirk and not a deeply disturbing and disgusting abnormality. They should have dealt with him the first time he touched a girl, the same way my parents should have dealt with Joey when he poured scalding hot oil over our nanny as a child because she dared to say no to him.

Lauren's silently sobbing face flashes into my mind, and I'm reminded they're all as bad as each other.

I continue scrolling through the slew of unread messages until I find one from Atticus himself. My finger hovers for a second before I finally open it up. I don't attempt to hide it or shy away from where Aodhan is reading over my shoulder because—

because we're together in this, no matter what happens.

Even if Atticus has been betraying us all.

I need to speak to you, Avery. Urgently.

Aodhan tries to get me to go back to sleep after I arrange a time and place to meet Atticus but there's no way I can relax now. I text Illi to borrow some clothes from Odie so when the sun finally starts to rise, Aodhan drives me the short distance over to the warehouse to change.

Odie's fashion sense is very different to mine but still impeccable.

We find a dress that drapes nicely and a pair of heels that are only one size bigger than I am so I can make them work. Odie's belly has doubled in size in the last week since I saw her, and I take a photo of the happy couple to send to Lips.

I'm going to have it framed and hung on my staircase back at the ranch with the rest of the family photos as well.

When we turn to leave, Illi stops me. "Wait here for a second, kid."

Then he jogs out of the apartment and down the stairs. I frown at Odie—is this a security thing?—but she smiles and rubs at her belly. *"He has a gift for you, la Reine."*

A gift.

From the Butcher of the Bay, that could be anything.

Aodhan smiles at Odie, a little strained because he's still

mildly terrified of what Illi will do to him if he thinks he's trying to flirt, and he obviously can't speak French so he has no idea about what we're saying.

"If it's a body part, I need some warning. I'll need to prepare myself so I don't upset Illi by running screaming from the house."

She throws her head back and laughs, the kind of laugh that lights up a room and calls out to the man who bled out a city to find her and sure enough Illi stomps back through the door with a box in his hands and the softest smile a man like him can manage.

He still looks like a brute.

"If there's a head in that box, we aren't friends anymore, Illi."

He laughs just a bit too hard at that, and Aodhan cuts me a look.

I really need to stop making Nate references around him until I speak to Lips about telling him. I still haven't decided if it's a good idea or not to tell him. The more people who know, the more chances there are for leaks and Posey is still only fifteen.

Her safety is our priority, and it has very little to do with the fact that Nate would go on a murderous rampage if anything happened to her.

Illi sets the box down on the table and flips the lid on it. "I would never give you body parts; I know you better than that. I got you some new toys and if you're going to confront that asshole Crawford, I need you to have some knives to throw at his throat if he starts his shit."

Aodhan glances down at me. "You know how to throw knives? What else is in your skill set that I don't know about."

Illi chuckles. "Don't tell him that shit. You gotta keep him guessing, keep him on his toes until he's smart enough to put a ring on your finger."

Jesus H Christ. "I know your aim is to embarrass the life out of me, but I'm not Lips and I'm above that bullshit. Thank you for the gift; I should really start carrying more weapons."

Aodhan takes the box and I kiss Odie's cheek as I pass her, giving Illi a quick hug even if he is a complete shit-stirrer. I imagine this is what having an older brother would be like in a normal family and… I'm oddly grateful for it.

Even with his arms full of the box, Aodhan still opens my car door for me and tucks me into the Impala. I send Lips a check-in message, just so she knows where I am and what our plans are because I feel like I'm about to be snatched off of the street.

It's stupid but I can't shake the feeling.

The fishing docks are enough of a drive away that I can go through the photos again and try to decide what I think is happening. If he can't explain it to me now then… then maybe it really is time to cut him free.

I can't bring myself to actually say it though.

When we pull into the parking lot, Atticus' car is already there waiting. I prepare myself to have to face Luca again, but when the driver's side door opens, Atticus himself steps out.

He's come alone.

Aodhan gets out of the car, and I wait for him to open my door for me, specifically because I know it will piss Atticus off and, sure enough, he stares Aodhan down like he's plotting out his murder.

They're so different.

Standing this close together here it's so unbelievably obvious how different they really are and yet I crave them both the same.

Atticus is wearing his usual charcoal suit, pressed and dry cleaned to perfection, with a pair of Hermes leather shoes. The crisp white shirt he's wearing under the suit jacket covers his tattoos I've only managed to get a peek at and he's wearing, as always, the Rolex I bought for him years ago.

Aodhan is wearing jeans and a tee with a jacket thrown overtop like he couldn't care less what he's wearing. With the same biker boots every Mounty I've ever met has an obsession for, he looks as though he's ready to wade into a street fight or a party by the docks, further down the coast from where we're now standing.

I stay tucked into Aodhan's side.

Atticus's jaw flexes as he grinds his teeth. "Avery, I asked to meet so I could speak privately with you."

Aodhan tenses but I shrug effortlessly, as though this is nothing to me despite my heart attempting to beat its way out of my chest. "You should have been clearer when you messaged;

I don't trust you enough right now to be here alone with you. There's too many unanswered questions."

His eyes narrow at me. "You mean other than you disappearing from my property in the middle of the night and then ignoring my calls? I had to call the Coyote to find out that you were safe."

Aodhan stays silent, thankfully, but the two of them still glare at each other like they're each waiting for the other person to make a wrong move.

It's infuriating.

I need answers.

"Why is my brother's photo tacked to the wall of your basement with his eyes crossed out? Harley, Blaise, Lips, half the O'Cronin family. Illi, Harbin, Roxas, the Boar... the list goes on, Atticus. Why? And while we're on the subject of your basement, why is Bing down there?"

No one would be able to pick up that I've surprised him, but I know him far too well to miss the signs. Once upon a time I would've said I knew Atticus Crawford the same way I knew myself, except then I fell down his rabbit warren of lies.

"I'm not talking about this with him here, Avery."

I huff and squeeze Aodhan's hand. "Take me home, we're done here. I'm done. I'm not going to be lied to and manipulated anymore."

Atticus takes a step forward. "Avery, for Christ's sake, all I have done is protect you! Everything, *everything*, I have done since

I came to Mounts Bay has been a move to get you out from your father's house."

I step away from Aodhan and towards Atticus, my temper flaring. "You bought me, wasn't that enough? You said you were worried about Ash? Then why *the fuck* was his photo on that wall?"

"How could you think I'd want Ash dead? You think that lowly of me, that I'd kill your beloved, asshole of a twin brother? For fuck's sake, Avery!"

Absolutely not, I won't stand for him using that tone at me. "You stood and watched Lips have her leg shattered to pieces. You told me yourself that you knew all about what my father was doing to Ash. I'm sure that you wouldn't physically harm me, Atticus, but I'm not sure you have any other lines when it comes to my family."

It's bounced around in my head a hundred times since I stumbled across that wall in the basement, but I still haven't figured out a plausible answer. "Explain to me why Ash's photo was on that wall. Give me a good reason. And Harley, Blaise, Lips, Aodhan, Jack... these people are non-negotiable to me and you have them pinned up on your murder board with their eyes crossed out!"

Atticus takes a deep, ragged breath and steps forward, his face set like stone. Aodhan steps up to me again, his body slightly in front of mine like he's prepared to dive in front of a bullet.

Or stop Atticus from snatching me and running.

The look that Atticus throws at him is purely the Crow, the man who walked out of his privileged life and into Mounts Bay to win the Game and become one of the country's most feared crime lords.

I can't stick around for this, my heart is aching at how badly he's ruined everything for us.

I turn away from him, prepared for this to be the last time I ever meet with him.

"Amanda Donnelley has been sending those photos for months."

I freeze but when I don't turn around he continues, "She's either the person sending them to you as well, pretending to be the Collector, or she's working with someone else. I know you think she's nothing worth worrying about but, Avery, she's more dangerous than you'd ever think."

I finally glance back at him and he's finally looking at me, ignoring Aodhan altogether. "I've done a lot of things I'm not proud of, I've become the worst sort of monster, but some things are sacred and you, your family and your happiness included, are one of those things. I don't care how much he hates me, I would never harm Ash."

I turn back to the car, ready to head home and throw everything I have at finding and destroying Amanda *fucking* Donnelley.

Atticus calls out again, "All members of the Twelve have to sponsor at least one person into the Game. If the Wolf isn't going to come home for the fights then you'll have to name someone for her. The meeting is in two days, have your sponsors ready."

I give him a curt nod because I'm well aware of the rules, but Aodhan tenses again, glancing down at me. I shrug at him because we'll just find him some thug to throw in the same way Illi did for Lips the last time, but he lets out a sigh like the day just got infinitely harder for him.

I know the feeling.

The Ruthless

Chapter Five

Atticus
Three Years Ago

The curtains slowly begin to draw back and an awed quiet takes over the crowd. The recital happens every year with all of the students from the state's most prestigious schools dancing and the ticket sales going to charity. It's a high society event and one that every rich and powerful parent and Hannaford Alumn attends.

Everyone knows who the star of the show is.

The music starts and Avery appears on stage, as effortless and graceful as a queen, the long lines of her body making me feel like a creep because she's only seventeen.

Seventeen.

But there's no denying that she's gorgeous, the most beautiful girl I've ever laid eyes on, and the years of avoiding her have only made her transformation from a young and pretty girl into the stunning woman who has every eye on her as she spins and jumps on stage effortlessly.

It takes years of discipline and hard work to make those jumps look as easy as breathing.

The woman next to me starts murmuring to her husband and I cut her such an icy cold look that she shuts up immediately, leaning away from me in her seat like she can somehow escape my wrath.

I don't want anyone ruining this moment for me, the fraction of time that I have to just sit and soak Avery in while she's doing something she both loves and excels at. I can sit here and just watch her without having to worry about her seeing me and speaking to me because every time she does I get a little closer to cracking.

I can't afford to break down and tell her everything yet.

She's still under her father's control and until she turns eighteen there's nothing I can do without him sending a whole country's worth of legal action toward me.

Once she's eighteen there's only the illegal resources I'll have to worry about and as the Crow, I have more than enough of my own firepower to send back to him. Every favor I collect, every senator I buy off, every crime lord I bind to myself—all of it is to get Avery and Ash away from that man.

My chest tightens as the crescendo of the song breaks, Avery's spinning on the stage a perfect arc and her feet steady and sure as she lands her final jump.

She's the only dancer to receive a standing ovation.

She's the only dancer who is already skilled enough to dance on any stage in the world. That's a fact and has nothing to do with all of the ways that she owns every part of my past, present, and future.

I built my entire business and my life around being what Avery needs to get her out of the Beaumont Manor and away from the evils of her family. I've never once regretted that decision and I never will.

When the curtain closes and the lights come back on for the intermission I stand from my seat. I need to get out of here before Avery finds out that I'd even attended but there's still something left to finish up with.

I need to fulfill the favor the Wolf called in.

It takes a little too long to get out of the seating area because everyone gets up and makes a beeline to the facilities here. It might be an exclusive event but the entire building is packed out with teachers, parents, and siblings. When I finally make it out, I head straight for the bar, immediately spotting the real reason I'm here. I shuffle through the crowd until I reach where Senior is standing by the bar, a bourbon and ice in his hand.

"Here he is, the useless Crawford boy ready to run me off again. What have you concocted this time to keep me away from my own children?"

I unbutton my jacket as I look around for Ash or any of his friends, just in case I need full mobility in my arms. They always wait for Avery backstage after her performance, just in case Joey or Senior go looking for her, and it's working to my favor tonight.

"I don't need to concoct anything, Joseph, there's more than enough skeletons in your closet to do it for me."

He takes another sip at his bourbon, the same type Ash favors, and sets the glass down. Both of his security guards are eyeing me like they're ready to take me out but anyone who willingly takes money from this man deserves to die screaming.

Maybe someday they will.

Probably at Joey's hands, the little freak never really cared who he was torturing just so long as they screamed.

"You have enough skeletons of your own. How long are we going to play this game, Crawford? How long are you going to keep panting after that girl? It's disgusting really, but it keeps me entertained. I enjoy watching you fall deeper and deeper into a life of crime to save her."

I shrug. "As long as you're entertained you're too busy to hurt her and that's all I care about. Playing with little girls is beneath you, pick some harder game."

His eyes are like icy cold voids, nothing behind the blue depths of them but a man who feels nothing. Truly, nothing. Most killers are made, something in their childhood or early teens breaks them until they're able to inflict that kind of pain onto others.

Senior was born with no soul.

Nothing.

"A shipment of fresh meat was delivered in DC by an old

friend of mine. Three of them are to your tastes and I've already booked you a room at the Oakridge."

It's my least favorite way of making this man disappear, but I learned a long time ago that there's nothing I wouldn't sacrifice to keep Avery safe. He knows it too, it's there in the little triumphant look on his face because he knows how much it costs me to hand other girls over to him to spare Avery from his sick little fantasies. It's enough that he'll go along with it… for now.

I'll need to up my game for the next time they're due to cross paths.

He finishes off the last of his drink and stands, buttoning up his suit jacket in that old money way that can't be taught, only bred into you.

I have it as well, though I'm nowhere near as proud of it as my peers. I stand there and watch him walk away, prepared to follow him out just to be sure he actually leaves without seeing his children.

"Oh, Crawford? Wherever did your brother disappear to? Bingley had just negotiated a price for Avery and then suddenly he was gone. You wouldn't happen to know anything about that, would you? Your father was talking about his stay in Thailand again and jogged my memory, but it's unusual for him to cut off all communication like that."

The smirk he throws over his shoulder as he speaks is dangerous, sharp, and knowing.

I'm dead if my father finds out where he is.

Chapter Six

Aodhan talks me into staying at the loft with him for a few more days, just until we have more of a handle on the Amanda Donnelley situation. I'm still convinced that a knife in the dark is all we need to get rid of the bitch, but until we find out where she sleeps, I have to be a little more cautious.

We stop off at my ranch to pack some bags so I don't have to keep raiding Odie's wardrobe to stay decent. I'd love nothing more than to spend some time shopping and replacing everything, nothing ever beating the feeling of crisp, clean, and new, but we don't have the time for that.

Between all of the research and prep for the Game and now sifting through all of the Crawfords' dirty laundry until I find out how the fuck Amanda fits into the picture, I'm going to be very busy.

I hand a giant box of file and paperwork to Aodhan and he grunts as he takes it. "Fucking hell. What do you need all of this for?"

I scoff at him and start filling a second box. "That's just barely half of it. We could just stay here if this is too much."

He huffs and starts up the stairs and out of my panic room. "This place is on too many psychopath's radars for my liking. Let's wait until a few more of them are dead before you come back."

I roll my eyes at him but at least he's not ordering me around about it. Lips had totally agreed about going back to the loft and Illi is happy we're finally a little closer to him and Odie in case anything else happens.

I force myself to only pack four bags of clothes and shoes, and then I text Atticus to have the bags I'd left behind there ready for me to collect after the next meeting. Aodhan offers to go pick them up for me, but I'm positive that's just asking for trouble.

When we get back to the loft, Aodhan is enough of a gentleman to do five trips to and from the car to get all of my luggage out. I immediately start a new murder board on his wall, this time in clusters because we finally have some leads.

Once I have the entire wall filled up, I start going back through the paperwork, most of it from Jackson but there's a few files from Atticus as well.

The Lily Heart Killer is hanging over my head like an executioner's blade.

I've thought about that file and what it means that Atticus is looking into Nate a hundred times over the last few weeks and it always boils down to the same thing; if Atticus goes after Nate, I'll have no choice but to side with my family over him.

Aodhan grabs a box of cookies, his sweet tooth far too obvious to me these days than ever before, and joins me on the floor.

"I'm more of an action guy but I'll read until my eyeballs bleed if that'll help you."

I shrug at him and try not to cringe at the thought of crumbs. "I'm not sure it'll be any help. I'm not exactly looking for something specific. It's... I'm looking for things that don't... feel right? I know that doesn't make sense, but it's the only way I can explain it."

He nods and gestures at the file. "What doesn't feel right about that one?"

The entire freaking file. "This is something Atticus gave me. He thinks... he thinks someone close to my family is the Lily Heart Killer. I disagree but mostly on principle, so I just keep reading it like maybe something will pop out."

He frowns. "Who else in your family could be a serial killer? Wait, that's a stupid fucking question. I doubt there's anyone who hasn't killed three or more people."

I grin at him. "Me. I haven't done that, though technically I've signed off on dozens of kills. I just don't want to ruin my nails or worse, my shoes."

He grins at me and leans over to kiss my neck, right under my ear. It's such an intimate and affectionate thing, something so sweetly him that I have to fight off a blush. I'm *not* the swooning type.

I leave that to Lips.

I let Aodhan go through the paperwork with me, his questions and comments more helpful than I thought they'd be but we're not really getting anywhere new. Atticus is either telling the truth and Amanda Donnelley is the biggest bad on the board right now.

Or he's lying, and believing him will get my brother killed.

I'm still poring over emails from Jackson about leads for Amanda's main location when Aodhan speaks again, startling me because I had forgotten he was even here with me in my concentration.

He's lying on the ground with his hands tucked behind his head, staring up at the wall.

"There's an awful lot of bikers up there. Any particular reason for that?"

I really don't want to lie to him. It feels inherently wrong to be in a relationship with someone you care so strongly for and to lie to them about something so big. I could argue that it's for his own safety, but really it's not.

It's for Poe's.

If I don't tell him, does that mean I think he'd tell people? Does it mean that I don't trust him? Fuck.

Fuck.

"I'm working on about forty different projects at once. The

Unseen and the Chaos Demons are one of those projects."

Aodhan nods and points his toe at one of the pictures. "He looks familiar... haven't seen him around the Bay in years though, I thought he was dead."

King Callaghan definitely isn't dead, I've had him stalked in federal prison from the moment Posey had said 'Unseen MC' back in the hospital. "He's the president of the MC down in Coldstone. I'm going to get him out of prison."

Aodhan's eyes narrow. "Why?"

That's an easier question to answer. "The entire club is riddled with spies and moles. The first step to getting the club out of trouble is getting their president out of prison and back home at the club."

Aodhan looks up at me with a frown. "I thought the Boar wasn't family? Did he hand a diamond over or something?"

"I don't want to lie to you but there's not a lot I can tell you. This isn't for the Boar, this is for someone very important to our family. The moment I can tell you, I will."

He stares at me for a second and then lets out a slow breath. "I guess that's all I can ask for. Are you safe? Is it a risk to you?"

"Not that I'm aware of. I think we're all safer the quicker I can clean that club out. Being thousands of miles away doesn't help with things and finding spies is almost impossible from this sort of distance."

Aodhan sits up and starts looking through the photos on the wall again. "I might actually be able to help with that. You know the Demons spend a lot of time down here at the docks right? The fishing side of town though. They're around a little less these days but they used to be here every other fucking month."

I did know that but I didn't realize he'd see much of them. "Illi did say he'd seen them there. His loyalties are mostly Silver City Serpents and a few of the local Unseen."

"Those two assholes we met at his place? Yeah, they don't seem all that fucking great. Who's this guy? He's... familiar."

He's pointing out Luis Martinez, the president of the Shreveport Unseen charter. "Another Unseen president. You recognize him?"

He nods. "I've seen him around. I've seen way too much of Grimm and his boys too, is that why you were asking about them?"

I nod, because it's easier than trying to find a truth I can say without sending myself spiraling again.

"Is there anything... specific you need to know? Other than who the rats are in the Unseen?"

I glance back over to him but his face is open and sincere. He wants to help me with this even though I won't give him more than the barest of details.

I stare up at Grimm Graves' face for a second and still feel the same mix of thankful and loathing. Thankful that I have Lips, but ready to gut that man for every last one of his many sins.

I think I could even do it myself.

"I need to know everything I can about Grimm. I need to know his plans, where he spends his days, how he runs his club, if he has a regular slut in his bed… I need to know what he eats for breakfast. I need everything about him."

Aodhan purses his lips a little. "I'll see what I can do, Queenie."

Our secluded time at the loft can only last for so long before our responsibilities come knocking.

I don't have anything pressing to do, other than ensuring I answer messages from my family checking in so they don't send the calvary after me, but the O'Cronin family need to see the head of the family occasionally and Aodhan needs to check in over some work they're due to do for the Boar.

I'm expecting him to leave me here to my work, but the moment we wake up wrapped up in each other, naked and warm, he murmurs to me to get myself moving because we have places to be.

I feel weirdly nervous.

Mostly because I've spent years of my life loathing the very idea of the O'Cronins. They had destroyed Harley's family and were the biggest threat to taking him out. They'd stolen my mother's money, his rightful inheritance, and were blackmailing him to force him into a life he didn't ever want.

They were messing with my family and I don't take that

lightly, not then and certainly not now.

I realize that the men responsible for all of that are now dead thanks to Aodhan and Jack cleaning house but there's still something... *wrong* about going there in broad daylight and making nice.

I'd been to visit Aodhan there once, at night, with Harley guarding me like I was a prized and delicate courtesan. I barely saw a thing and besides Jack, I wouldn't have even known Aodhan had family there.

This feels too important so I obsess and fuss like only I can.

I pick out my most Beaumont outfit that I'd packed. A Chanel skirt, blouse, white blazer with pearl buttons, and a pair of Louboutins to finish it off. I curl my hair and do a full face of makeup. I haven't been this polished in weeks, probably since the Morrisons' charity ball, and it's soothing to me.

I know how to be this version of myself.

Aodhan takes in every inch of me with appreciation but doesn't comment about just how far overboard I've gone, thankfully, he just helps me down the stairs and then tucks me safely into the Impala.

When we make it over to the compound, he helps me back out of the car and holds out a hand, threading his fingers through mine when I take it. There's no hesitance in him at all, no part of him that seems nervous to be bringing me here to meet his entire family.

Well.

The surviving members of his family.

I met his father and his grandfather at the Game, all the way back in the very first round when he had stepped in to take a chance at becoming a member of the Twelve. I remember just how worried Harley had been, how he'd been furious at an O'Cronin entering and having a chance to sit at that table.

I think he'd been worried about Aodhan dying too. He would never have admitted it back then but Harley had never spoken badly of his fraternal cousins. When it came to his uncles and grandfather, he would drag them through the mud at every opportunity, but his cousins were never spoken about.

That's more telling than anything he could have said.

The O'Cronins' compound is actually not at all a compound. Once upon a time it was one of Mounts Bay's very first gated communities and all of the houses were owned by the Irish family. I'm sure it would have been a beautiful place to live back when my Aunt Iris had moved in but under the tyrannical rule of Liam the entire place is... disgusting.

Aodhan scoffs at the wrinkle in my nose and leans down to kiss it. "Believe it or not, we've already cleaned it up. A lot."

I can't imagine anything that would be worse than this.

Aodhan chuckles at me under his breath and then starts to point things out to me like the repairs that are happening to the roof of one house and the garden beds that are now nothing but dirt but were once, apparently, overgrown and full of Liam's cigarette butts.

I hate him even more.

"The work at the docks has gone a long way to getting everything back on track. We owe the Wolf a lot."

He always reverts back to calling Lips by her Twelve name, a sign of respect to her I'm sure but still a little jarring for me considering how much they both mean to me.

I shrug and try not to fixate on the bullet holes in the side of the house. "She would've helped you even if you weren't Harley's cousin, you know. It would have cost you a favor, but Lips is a good person… most of the time."

I feel the need to tack that on the end because there isn't a person in the Bay who isn't aware that she's an assassin for hire. I'm not sure you can call a killer a good person, but she is. She's the best person, her moral code is just a little skewed compared to others.

It's his turn to shrug. "We still owe her. It's only going to take another couple of months before everything will be paid off and fixed completely."

I nod. It says a lot about how proud he is of everything they've managed to achieve since he became a member of the Twelve. He's the leader the family should have had in the first place, the type of man who does the right thing, no matter the cost to himself.

It makes me proud to call him mine.

When we walk up the path to Aodhan's house, I can see it's had the least work done to it so far. The gardens need work and the bullet holes from the shooter who'd left that photo of us in the Jackal's lair are still there, no attempts to repair them.

He slides his keys in and gives me a half-smile over his shoulder. "I'm barely here anymore; I've been more worried about getting the loft ready in case we needed it while your family was away."

I take a second to rein myself in, just in case the place is disgusting on the inside. I don't want to be rude and run screaming into the streets because his housekeeping isn't great.

Deep breath, I follow him in. He flicks the lights on as we go through the hall and into the modest kitchen. Everything is scrubbed clean, so even though nothing has been updated in at least thirty years, it's not so bad. The tiled flooring has some cracks in it and there's a few patches on the walls.

"This was the family home. It's taken a while to fix all of the shit Domhnall broke."

I nod and find myself drawn over to the very few photos on one of the walls in the kitchen. There's one of Aodhan and Cara as children. There's one of his mother. I almost miss Harley in the photo of all of the O'Cronin cousins.

He'd have to be only five or six in it, back when Éibhear was still alive and Aunt Iris was still whole. The grin on his face is so sweet and innocent, the kind that Ash and I never had the chance to have with Joey's torture in our childhood.

I snap a photo of it and send it to him.

Then I send one to Ash, then Lips.

Neither of the guys message me back, but Lips requests a copy for the family wall and one for herself. I have to admit, I want one printed and left in my room where I can see his happy face every day. A reminder that underneath the hulking asshole exterior, my cousin was once a very happy and loved little boy.

I want Liam dead all over again.

"I used to be very jealous of Harley. So fucking jealous, it's almost embarrassing now to think of it,"Aodhan says, a pile of mail in his hands that he's flicking through. Something so mundane while we discuss the horrors of life in the Bay.

I glance over at him to meet his eyes and he gives me a rueful smile. "Éibhear fucking loved him. Iris too, they both thought he'd hung the moon. He was always clean and fed and loved, no matter what else was going on around here. Plus he was like looking at fucking sunshine, always grinning and happy. I couldn't help but wish I had that too."

"I would've felt the same way. My... my mother was like that with Ash and I. She shielded us from a lot, favored us and spoiled us. She knew there was something wrong with Joey though. The day she was killed she was trying to run. She had every intention of leaving Joey behind after what he did to Ash."

He nods along as I tell him the entire, gruesome story. It only seems fitting to be telling him something so personal and revealing while standing in a house filled with the ghosts and ghouls of his own traumatic childhood.

I can't give him all of the secrets I keep, but I can give him my own truths and hope that it's enough. The moment the whole story is out, I feel like I've aged ten years, utterly exhausted in a matter of seconds.

He slings an arm around my shoulders and shoves the envelopes into his back pocket. "C'mon, Queenie. Let's go see the family and get out of here before anything else gets dragged out of us."

I meet too many people too quickly. It's loud and it's chaotic and Aodhan stays glued to my side the entire time like he's afraid I'm going to run screaming from the gated community.

I'm wearing heels; there's no way he'd lose me.

The important thing is that I learn that no matter how I've built the O'Cronin clan up in my head, they're just a family. A rough and loud and completely insane family.

Harley would've fitted right in.

Chapter Seven

I wake up to a phone call from Lips, her ringtone cutting through the air and startling me upright until I find my phone in the sheets.

Aodhan barely grunts and rolls over.

"What's happened? Are you okay?" I whisper, pulling myself out of the bed and stalking over to the bathroom so I won't wake Aodhan.

"Fuck, what time is it there? This isn't an emergency, everything is fine… well, not fine because Finn's bus got a flat and now he's sharing with us while it's getting fixed, and our bus isn't big enough for the five of us."

I snort at her and perch my ass on the rim of the bathtub. "You mean you haven't been able to have your nightly orgies and your idiot boys are grumpy over the blue balls? That's rough. I'm sorry."

She giggles at me and I roll my eyes. She's definitely drunk. I'm happy for her and sad for my plan of eight hours of sleep that just flew out of the window.

"I miss you."

She sighs. "I miss you too. I should have just texted you this information but I wanted to hear your voice. Fuck, I sound like a creep but yeah. I don't want to go on tour again without you."

I giggle at her honesty, all of the things she'd never let herself say without the whiskey softening her up. "We have four years of college to do after the tour, we'll be sick of each other by the end of that."

She snorts and I can hear male voices arguing behind her. It's someone I don't recognize and I think Blaise but the shouting and bad line makes it hard to tell. "Impossible. If I ever move out of the ranch I'm buying the house next door. How much will that cost me? Wait, don't tell me. My stomach hurts and I don't wanna puke at how much your place cost you."

I laugh at her because she's being cute as hell and then I cringe at how loud I'm being.

Being in a relationship is weird.

"Okay, what's the information you need to give me before we get distracted completely?" I say, squirming a little because this isn't a comfortable place to sit at all.

"Right, right. Sorry. Illi put word out that we're open to sponsoring someone for the Game. He got a few hits back but they were all fucking bad so I was starting to think I'd have to sweet talk Illi into taking a spot but then we got a call from a girl."

My eyebrows raise. "I thought you said you didn't want to put a girl in after what happened during the last games."

And what a mess that had been. None of them were trained or prepared in any way, and they all had a death wish which is fine, it's their own lives, but there's something about a girl in the ring that makes or breaks men.

Every last one of them died horrific deaths.

"This one... this one is different. Her name is Lucia Ammoscato but she goes by Lucy—"

"Wait, Ammoscato? She's related to the Lynx?" I cut in. There's no way I'd ever forget the details of that disgusting woman, even after Nate cut her head off for attempting to double cross his sister.

She was also a cougar whore who had her eye on Harley.

"Yep, her niece. The mafia family always have someone in the Twelve, but they've already picked out their male heirs they want in the fold and they've struck a deal with the Bear to have them both sponsored. They think they can both win and take the two open seats."

I scoff, because isn't that typical male bullshit. "So she's shopping around trying to go up against them? Why would we want to sponsor her?"

There's the sounds of a door opening and then closing, a lock sliding into place. The only place on the bus with a lock is the tiny bathroom so I guess this is just where we both have these conversations now.

"She didn't shop around, she called me first. She had a whole speech prepared of what her intentions are and what she's going to owe the family if we do choose to take her up."

Huh.

"She fucking hated her aunt and half her cousins. She's a couple of years older than us but I remember her from a couple of parties at the docks I went to. Honestly... my money is on her and I'd take her over the other Ammoscatos any day of the damn week."

That sounds reasonable enough but I need to dig through this Lucy's entire life before I'm comfortable putting her forward. When I tell Lips that she doesn't argue at all. "If you find any red flags, gimme a call and we can decide if it's a deal breaker or not. You know we're in this together, no matter what."

I fucking adore her. "I'll get onto Jackson and Illi now, if she's genuine then she's our best option. Having another member who owes us and will side with us will be handy."

She hums under her breath. "That's what I want, a majority rule that we can have up our sleeves when shit goes down. There's been some talk about getting the skin auctions opened again and, honestly, I don't fucking want that to happen. Beyond how fucking disgusting they are, Illi will lose his mind. I think he's waited to start a family until that shit was dealt with."

I groan quietly. "Let me guess, the Bear wants that to be his new start? I think we should kill him. If we do it now we won't have to worry about running another Game because this is time consuming. Who knew running the biggest crime syndicate in the country would have so many traditions and rules we'd have to follow."

Lips chuckles at me. "Remember in high school when we'd do everything we could not to have to kill people? How times change."

I huff at her, "Is that a yes? I'm taking it as a yes, Illi will be thrilled. He loves adding to his Twelve death toll."

"Better the member we know than some new blood trying to prove a point. We can reassess if it looks like he's actually going to start the skin markets again."

She sounds sober again and I hate that all of this work talk has ruined her buzz. If anyone deserves to let their hair down it's Lips Anderson.

"Go fuck one of your boys on the couch or something, enjoy the rest of your night. I love you, don't do anything I wouldn't do."

She laughs a little too loud. "I love you too, go climb back into bed with your Irishman and do something that would enrage your brother. You deserve it."

I laugh at her and slip back out of the room, trying to quietly slip back into bed without disturbing Aodhan. The moment I get between the sheets he pulls me into his body with a little grunt.

"What's happened now?"

I giggle quietly at the affront in his voice. "Nothing but we have a candidate for the Game. Go back to sleep; I'll work quietly. Scout's Honor."

He mumbles under his breath at me, a lot to say about how I've clearly never been a Girl Scout, and then he slips out of the bed and into the bathroom.

Illi messages me back straight away, ready to dig into Lucy's trash cans if that's what it takes to vet her. Jackson takes a little time but when he does get back to me he promises to have a file to me in a matter of hours.

There's a Twelve meeting tonight.

I was starting to get a little concerned that we wouldn't have anyone to name and Atticus would have a complete blow up over it. We'd done the same last time, waited until the very first round of fighting before we threw in the street rat Illi had found.

We still have to find someone for Aodhan.

When he crawls back onto the mattress I mention this to him and even in the darkness of the loft I see him cringe. "I already have someone. Jack wants to enter."

My eyes snap over to him, and he lets out a deep breath like he's been holding it in for months. "He's been fucking suicidal since Myra. I don't... I don't think he wants to make it out alive."

Jesus H. Christ. "So what are you going to do?"

He rubs a hand over his face. "I told him I wouldn't put him in if he was just going there to die but he said he had more pride than that. I guess he just wants to flirt with death. If I can win it, he can too."

That doesn't make me feel any better.

The background checks all come up with nothing.

Twenty pages of information from Jackson that all boil down to the fact that Lucy doesn't play well with others... but only when provoked. The thing is, her cousins have all provoked her a lot and there's tons of evidence on the Lynx trying to punish the girl.

Illi only had one thing to say about her.

"She's a raging fucking psycho. We should definitely bring her on board."

I roll my eyes at him, because of course he'd love a little more psycho sitting at the table, but I ask Aodhan to drop me off at Illi's warehouse so we can ride over together to the meeting with Lucy. She picked the restaurant and the time, and I'd only agreed because they would've been my choices too. It's not my absolute favorite dining choice, but Illi will be able to find a steak or burger to murder and they do a great takeout option for him to grab for Odie when we leave.

We arrive early for Illi to scope out the place before we go in. I've already checked all of the cameras and the guest list for the night, nothing flagged for me and because no one knows about our association with Nate or the fact that the Devil was the one cutting people's heads off last year, I'm not too worried about this meetup.

Lucy needs something from us.

If she attempts to hurt either of us, the Wolf would come for her. It offers us an extra layer of protection.

Not that the hulking, murderous serial killer sitting next to me needs it.

"Are you wearing your knives? I didn't get them to decorate the Stag's safe house, Queenie."

I roll my eyes at him. "Yes, I'm aware of that and actually I am wearing them. I wore this jacket specifically to hide them, didn't you notice? It's far less tailored than my usual white blazer."

He looks at me like I'm speaking Spanish and *el no entiende*.

"I have the throwing stars and some knives. The gun is in my purse, cleaned and loaded. I made Aodhan check it before he dropped me off just to be sure."

He grunts and nods his head, still not happy but satisfied enough to drop the issue. He gets out and I wait for him to come open my door, even though I really could do it myself. There's something about being Avery Beaumont that has all of the men around me ready to open doors. I always thought it was a money and class issue but now I suppose it's a respect thing. Illi does it because he knows how much I mean to our family and it's the best way to keep me close.

After we're shown to our table, I take my seat and place a napkin over my legs. Illi immediately picks up a menu and I watch the relief roll into his body that the food here is real and edible.

Hannaford has scarred the man for life.

"Do you know what this chick looks like? I didn't bother asking anyone for details because I don't fucking care about that shit."

I laugh at him and flag a waiter down for some drinks because a wine to take the edge off is exactly what I need right now. Plus, it'll make Lucy think we're far more relaxed about this meeting than I really am. "I'll let you know when she gets here, don't worry, you just focus on picking which sauce you want for your steak."

He scoffs at me and then grumbles under his breath about the cost. I roll my eyes at his dramatics and pick out the salmon dish for myself. We won't actually eat anything until Lucy joins us, we're not total heathens, but there's not much else to look at around the room that we haven't already seen in the security cameras.

I notice the moment she arrives.

She comes through the back entrance which isn't a red flag, because there's private parking back there, and she makes eye contact with me from across the room, just barely dipping her head in a sign of respect but one that she seems to struggle with.

I can handle that.

Maybe she does have the backbone to survive the Game, because skill will only get you so far. Well, it'll get you through the first few rounds, designed entirely to weed out the weakest of the bunch, but the later rounds?

You need to have a brain to survive.

I've had a lot of input into the Game this time around. We can't completely rig the competition so our own picks win, not this time around anyway, but there are ways we can make it more favorable and the final rounds are exactly that.

There's no way any of the meathead brawlers that the Viper has sponsored will ever beat the later rounds. I can feel it in my goddamn bones, so much so that I'd wager my entire fortune on it.

I nudge Illi and he looks up to take a long, hard look at Lucia Ammoscato and make his final assessment.

She looks exactly like the raging fucking psycho he promised me.

The restaurant isn't a black tie establishment but the leather jacket, black corset and pants that are so tight, I have a great deal of respect for her for managing to get into them.

She's also wearing thigh high boots over them, the silver clasps on them matching the silver jewelry draped over her. The only part of her that isn't dark and screaming murderous goth girl is her white blonde hair, natural and curling slightly like she did put time and effort into it.

She's beautiful and not at all a wallflower. She smirks as she crosses the room, completely at ease with every eye in the room following her and making harsh judgments about her. I can basically see their opinions bouncing off of her like they're nothing.

I might like this girl.

I might even want her to win the Game just so I can watch her shake that table of misogynistic assholes up.

She takes the seat across from Illi and I, moving the menu away and flicking a hand out to attract a waiter. She's been here before, clearly, and orders both her drink and food. We do the same and then there's a moment of silence before she finally speaks.

"You're much prettier than I imagined. I was expecting some posh, stuffy bitch the way my aunt talked about you."

Maybe I don't like her. "Your aunt was a disgusting, manipulative, dense bitch. She got the death she deserved and if you can't handle that truth then we're done here."

The smirk on her face widens. "She sure did. There's no need for dramatics; I'm here to discuss what I can do for you in return for my sponsorship. I heard you didn't want the skin auctions to open again."

I tilt my head in her direction, a nod without actually doing it. There's too many eyes and ears around, and I've slipped back into the upper class skin I'm most protected in.

Illi isn't so concerned. "That's one of the conditions, if we sponsor you and you're successful. You vote it down, no matter the cost to you."

She smirks a little, lifting her glass to her lips and taking a sip. The black lipstick smears a little on the rim and when she sets it back down she leans forward to murmur quietly to us.

"I understand the risk the Wolf and the Family are taking on by sponsoring me. I'm a risk, I'm from poor breeding stock, and there's bad blood. I have no interest in joining your little band of merry little sheep, but I will always pay my debts. Consider this a token of my appreciation."

I straighten a little in my seat but Lucy's eyes flick over to the corner of the restaurant. Illi's eyes follow hers and curses under his breath.

He leans down to whisper to me, his voice barely more than a breath, "That's D'Camillo. He's made a name for himself as a 'wholesaler'. Brings in thousands of girls a year to the auctions, all of them taken off of the streets."

I give him a curt nod then say to Lucy, "Giving him to us will definitely do as a peace offering. We look forward to working with you."

Her smirk gets wider and she waves a hand at me in dismissal. "I would never give such a gift. It's impolite to give people more work to do."

There's a crash and then a scream, and I look over to find D'Camillo gasping and choking on the ground, his hands clawing at his neck as he convulses and foams at the mouth.

Poison.

Illi sighs and nudges our plates away from us, looking mournfully at the steak untouched on his. "We forgot the cardinal rule. Fastest way to take someone out is to poison their vices."

I giggle at him and watch Lucy who still hasn't torn her eyes away from where two waiters are still attempting first aid on D'Camillo.

"Good thing I have none."

Chapter Eight

One day I'm going to have to look into couture bulletproof fabrics.

I didn't pack anywhere near enough clothing so Aodhan drives me back over to my ranch to get ready for the meeting, waiting downstairs for Illi to arrive.

Strapping the Kevlar vest to myself isn't difficult but finding something to wear over it that doesn't look ridiculously oversized or bulky is impossible. I'm forced to wear a dress and a blazer, neither of them the tight and deadly style I like, but Aodhan still stares at me as I walk down my staircase like he'd love nothing more than to find his way under the skirt so I must look decent enough.

It's also uncomfortable to move with so many weapons strapped to my body.

I'd promised Lips I wouldn't leave the house without at least three knives and a gun tucked into my purse, and at the time I didn't realize how constricting that would be for me.

As I walk down the staircase, I find Illi and Aodhan muttering between themselves about something, probably related to their hunting trip and about the photos but I can't force myself to think about that right now.

We have other things to deal with.

"You look uncomfortable as hell, Queenie," Aodhan says with a smirk, and Illi glances over his shoulder at me.

He grins and rolls his eyes at me. "Do you not trust me or something, kid? I got you that shit to use when I'm not around, just in case O'Cronin needs some backup or a warning shot. A gun and the vest will do."

I shrug. "I'm not ever going to be caught unaware again. What's the point in learning how to use all of this if I don't have it on me when I need it?"

Illi's eyebrows hit his hairline, a smirk stretching over his face. "Your brother isn't gonna know what the fuck to do with you when he gets home."

Aodhan grins at me and kisses my cheek as I get to the bottom of the stairs, murmuring in my ear, "I've gotta grab Jack; I'll see you guys there."

He squeezes my hand before we all head out, walking me to Illi's car and tucking me in safely before he climbs into the Impala and takes off.

"He's a good man. If you're going to choose between him and the Crow you know where my vote is going," Illi mumbles, starting the BMW up and pulling out.

I roll my eyes at him. "Good thing it isn't something that will be put to vote then, isn't it? Besides, Lips didn't have to choose. Who says I will?"

Illi snorts, weaving through what little traffic is on the road this late out and in my gated community. "Fuck, it's gonna end up being a family thing. I'm telling you all now, my dick belongs to my girl and my girl alone, and any man that touches her is bleeding the fuck out on the floor so we'll be the odd ones out."

I cackle at him because I can't imagine a world in which Illi and Odie ever thought of touching other people. I'm not like Lips, I'm not struggling at all with the idea of being with two men because… well, I've been honest with them both from the moment I met them. Aodhan has always known about Atticus and if my life-long love had've done something a little earlier then maybe I wouldn't even be considering this unconventional path.

Atticus might not want to share me.

I have to make peace with that.

Illi directs us through the traffic with ease and I find myself considering purchasing a BMW for how smoothly it eats up the road. I don't want to mention it to Illi, because he'll immediately start talking specs and messaging Ash and Harley to gloat about winning me over.

Car people are insane and I don't want to get thrown into an argument about useless shit like this.

The meeting is once again happening at the docks, the

warehouse where most of the famous Mounts Bay parties are also held, and when we pull up to the parking lot there's only a couple of dozen cars. The difference of getting out of the car and walking into the warehouse without the eyes of the Jackal's men on us is like a breath of fresh air.

Fucking blissful.

It looks desolate inside the warehouse without the writhing, practically naked bodies dancing around in the dark with only the strobe lights and drugs to keep them going. This is prime party season for the Bay so I'm a little surprised that there's nothing going on tonight. Even with the Jackal dead, the Fox is the one who actually organizes the party, so there's no real excuse for it being empty.

Atticus waits at the bottom of the stairs for us.

Illi huffs and glues himself to my side. "Crow, if I find out you're the one sending those fucking photos—"

Atticus cuts him off. "Whoever is sending them knows about the Chaos Demon's connection. Colt's photo arrived on my doorstep this morning, Lips was in it. I called her to warn her that she's being watched, but she already knew. Amanda has definitely stepped up her little game and has a tail on all of us now; I suggest you all think very carefully about your movements until we have this under control."

Jesus H. Christ.

Illi curses under his breath and steps away from me, his phone at his ear as he calls Odie. There's no way he left her without guards for the night, Harbin and Roxas at the very least, but there's a big difference between having guards because the Bay is a dangerous place and having guards because there's someone stalking you.

I'd bet money on whoever is watching Odie to be dead before the meeting is over.

I glance around but there's no one near us here. "Is Colt the only photo you got? None of the... others?"

I don't want to say Posey or Nate's names, just in case there is someone hiding somewhere who might hear their names.

Atticus knows exactly who I'm talking about. "There's no indication that she's going to focus on anyone else. I will tell you if there's a chance she's looking into anyone else. No matter how much I don't like any of this, Avery, I would never put them at risk. I know better than that."

I think I believe him.

Something seems to have changed with him, maybe something about me finding that wall has shaken him, and now he's at least giving me information and not heavily veiled warnings.

It's the most dangerous thing because I feel the first little rays of hope start deep in my belly where they can sprout wings and take over my life again. I try to talk myself down, he's hurt me before and he'll hurt me again, but those feelings don't just disappear.

They can't.

I understand now that my heart has the room in it for two men, and I won't ever feel complete without them both.

Atticus hesitates for a second and then holds out his arm for me to take. I glance back at Illi who still has his phone pressed tightly to his ear but he nods at me and stalks up behind us again, cutting the call off.

I take Atticus' arm.

The moment we get into the elevator I drop it and move back into Illi's side, completely aware that he's here for my protection and slinking away with Atticus just because of my traitorous heart will make that harder for him.

I also need to get my head into the game because distraction leads to missing important clues and cues, and I'm not having someone's death on my conscience.

Or my own.

When the doors open Atticus strides away and over to his seat, nodding at his men as he passes. Luca is there waiting for him, a somber look on his face even as he tips his head in my direction. Illi holds out his arm and I take it, letting him lead me in as we both look around at everyone with a cold indifference.

The table is round and worn and takes up a large portion of the room.

This is the same room that Lips had confronted the O'Cronin's at to get Harley free of Liam and Domhnall. She handed over a diamond to every member of the Twelve for their cooperation and I don't think Harley will ever get over that fact.

It doesn't matter that she still has dozens left, tens of millions of dollars stashed away in her little safe, all he can see in his head are those little velvet bags being handed over for his sake.

It's such a Mounty thing to worry about.

Aodhan's arm is slung over the chair next to his like he's saving it for me and Jackson is slouching in the next one down, so I'll be wedged between family.

Illi leads me over and tucks me into the table, every move respectful and like a taunt to the others sitting with me.

Go ahead. Try and touch her, see what I'll do to you.

Only the Butcher of the Bay could get away with that sort of thing and every time he thumbs his nose at them all, I freaking love him a little more. I understand completely why Lips would throw down for him any day of the week.

The Boar arrives last, a little blood-soaked and harried looking, but no one comments on it. Atticus just waits until we're all seated and then he starts with the usual list of issues and teething problems we're having in the city.

Still no updates on who is pushing the Jackal's product. Three men have been caught dealing and all three of them swallowed a cyanide tablet to kill themselves before they could be questioned.

That kind of loyalty to their employer... it's rare and it's dangerous.

"No markings on any of them?" I say, frowning a little and Jackson shrugs.

"I went over the coroner's reports. Nothing. Three dead guys in cheap suits, nothing worth reporting on."

Jesus.

I make a mental note to speak to Lips about it, because it doesn't sound right. Well, cyanide tablets never sound right but there's something decidedly not Mounts Bay about that.

I glance over my shoulder and the frown on Illi's face confirms it.

We finally move onto the real reason we're all here tonight.

"We have to put forward our nominees for the Game. If you have someone in mind, they have to be put forward tonight. If you don't put them down tonight, you can't throw them into the ring next week. Am I clear on that, Viper?"

The bookie grunts and waves a hand, notorious for changing rules as he sees fit. Last year he'd swapped out guys in the third round and had a screaming match with the Ox about it on the sidelines when his new guy won.

Atticus waits for any objections and when there are none, he starts to slowly call on each of the members to put their people forward.

The Fox looks around the table at each of us, the brightly colored tattoos etched into his aging skin a marker of the time and hard nature of being the party man. I wonder how many of the Jackal's drugs he's taken over the years or if he knew about the dirty batches he'd pass out to anyone he needed to disappear.

I wonder how much the Fox trusted his now dead accomplice.

"I have eight men to put forward."

Atticus nods and takes down their names as the Fox lists them off. None of the men ring any bells and by the look on Aodhan's face they mean nothing to him as well.

I'll ask Illi about them later, once Atticus gives me a copy of the notes.

The Bear has a seemingly endless list of men, including two of the Lynx's relatives, and I can't help but roll my eyes. He's trying to court some new friends and revive his destroyed business by having a new partner in the Twelve. Pathetic.

The Tiger has one man, someone Atticus arranged for him, and he looks as though this entire meeting is distasteful to him. I often wonder about his reasons for joining the Twelve and why he doesn't just take his fortune and leave. It's probably safe to do so now, I highly doubt anyone at this table currently would object.

Jackson names another of the Crow's picks, his Wolf tattoo flexing on the table as he picks at a bullet hole. He smirks when he notices me looking at it, wriggling his fingers in that chronically flirty way that he has. I'm convinced he doesn't even realize just how suggestive he is because I've seen how he is with Viola, but Aodhan leans forward in his seat to death stare at him.

Atticus refrains.

I actually respect him a little more for finally not interfering with what I do at this table on the Wolf's behalf, for not throwing himself in between me and any perceived threat.

These weak men are not a threat to me, not really, not now the Jackal is dead and everything that once was a sure thing in the Bay is yet again up in the air.

The Ox, the Boar, and the Viper each name a small handful of men. There aren't any women yet but I actually think that's a good thing, considering I don't really want to watch their deaths and I want Jack and Lucy to win.

"Stag, who are you nominating?" Atticus' eyes give nothing away and I'd be impressed if I weren't so sure he's plotting out Aodhan's death every second of the day.

"Jack O'Cronin."

The Bear scoffs and snaps, "More fucking family. Everyone is trying to fill the seats with allies."

I roll my eyes at him. "You put forward twenty-two men of your own. If anyone is trying to manipulate this process for their own gain, it's definitely you."

He turns on me with a curled lip and manic eyes that are just a little too Joey-esque for my liking. "There's never been a cap on nominees. Don't try to change the fucking rules now just to suit yourself. Some of us are real Mounties and enjoy a little bloodsport. Maybe you should go home to your gilded fucking castle and play pretend there."

What I wouldn't give to wipe this man off of the board.

Atticus doesn't interrupt for once. It's jarring because I'm so used to him throwing himself into every little interaction or argument, but he just sits there and waits until I'm done.

I take a deep breath.

"Your men will all be dead before the third round. If the Viper is running the books for the Game, I'll put money on it. You only won the Game because you went up against the weakest and most pathetic that the Bay had to offer, I'm sure of it, because how else would such a worthless excuse of a man be able to take a seat at this table?"

The Boar scoffs and says, "He went up against drug addicts and fucking pussies."

The Bear turns on him but finally Atticus interrupts, "Do you have any other nominees, Stag, or can we continue?"

Aodhan jerks his head at him sharply. "I'm only sponsoring one person: Jack's it."

Atticus looks over at me, his face still as blank as it always is during these meetings. "Who will the Wolf be putting forward?"

I meet his eyes across the table and I don't feel angry at him for the first time in months. "Lucia Ammoscato."

There's cursing in the crowd of men and Atticus's sharp, icy glare cuts through them until they shut the hell up. "Bear, if your nominees can't keep their mouths shut during meetings, they won't make it to the Game."

The Bear's lip curls in my direction again and there is nothing that would make me happier than wiping that man from the face of the Earth.

I consider calling Nate and paying him double to do it.

"The Wolf is once again trying to stir up shit! This is a

fucking vendetta against me!"

Atticus rolls his eyes, and Aodhan leans a little closer to me in his seat like he's prepared for the Bear to pull a gun. I'm wearing Kevlar under my clothing, so I'm less concerned. I doubt he's a good enough shot to actually manage to shoot me, and he'd be dead before the bullet left the chamber.

Illi's cleavers never miss.

I'm not afraid of the Bear. "If you've been dense enough to sponsor men who can only win under very specific circumstances... that's your own stupidity. I chose someone I thought would not only win but would be an asset at this table for us all."

Everyone turns to look at the Crow as if he'll try to reprimand me, but instead he just looks around the room slowly and then says, "I'm also only nominating one person. Luca Veltori."

I lock myself down fast so that the shock doesn't show on my face. I should've known Atticus would be putting forward someone to fill a seat who would be loyal to him, but now we have two seats available and three people that we want to win.

We can't afford to have them lose, not when the penalty is death.

No one says another word in protest, the meeting finally coming to a close, and I hold in everything I have to say, all the way down to the BMW. Aodhan catches my eye but when he sees the storm brewing there, he nods at Illi and walks with Jack out to the car.

I'll find my way back to him when I'm ready.

The moment Illi gets in and shuts his door he murmurs, "Is killing the Bear on the planner yet? We need the extra seat."

"I need to speak to Atticus."

Chapter Nine

I message Atticus to meet me, and he answers straight away with a location. I've never been out to that side of Mounts Bay before, but when I show it to Illi, he just gives me a curt nod and changes the direction of the car.

I also message Aodhan to tell him I'll be another few hours. He answers immediately, like he was poised and ready with a reply.

Tell the Crow I'll kick his front door in and set fire to the place if he tries to keep you again.

I want to be able to write something witty and cute back to him, but my stomach is still a riot of nerves. There's something telling me we need Lucy on our side, that she's going to be a valuable asset to our family in the Twelve but with only two seats available… Jack cannot lose. There's no way that Aodhan can lose him and, though we haven't exactly had all that much time together, he's been nothing but a loyal family member that I've seen.

I want more cousins for Harley.

I want him to come home and to find more people who love him and will support him. I want him to find that smiling boy from that photo again and I think Lips has helped with that, but maybe being able to spend time with the O'Cronins will do even more for him.

I can't lose Jack.

But Luca saved Lips' life. Pushing my own aversion to him aside, he saved her life and was a friend to her when she so desperately needed one. He's one of Atticus' most trusted confidants, and I'd wager that he's his closest friend.

Three people and two open seats, it's not going to work.

We pull into the suburb and it only takes another minute before Illi is parking up at a tiny park with a single bench. Atticus is already here, sitting there waiting for me, and I run a hand down my skirt as though that will fix the uncomfortable outfit I'm wearing.

"Do you need backup or is this more of a solo mission? Either way I'll have a gun aimed at his head."

I scoff at Illi and open my own door. "Solo, and I have the weaponry covered, remember? I'll be as quick as I can be; I know you need to get home to Odie."

He grins at me, his teeth pearly white under the streetlamp. "The tail on her is already dead. Same with Harbin and Roxas' guy. The minute they knew about them, they had them tracked down and gutted like rats. Do what you need to do; my girl is safe."

Thank God.

I nod at him, take a deep breath, and then step out into the cold night air. It's only a few hours before dawn and the grass has a layer of dew covering it, soaking the bottoms of my shoes in the most disgusting way.

I cringe my way through the short distance to the bench, taking a seat and looking out over the playground equipment in a mirror of Atticus' pose.

It's a quiet night out here.

"Things are only going to get worse, Floss."

I *refuse* to cry.

I will not.

"We need an extra seat, and I know who I'd prefer to lose from the table."

He nods slowly and then shifts in his seat, digging around in his pocket until he pulls out a small, black velvet bag.

A diamond.

"The Bear handed this over to me before the meeting. Called in a favor to ensure that we don't have him killed."

Motherfucker.

I look back out over the park because looking at Atticus still hurts too much. I'm not sure I'll ever be able to just look at him again, not outside of the Twelve meetings where he's not my Atticus anymore, he's the cold, cruel, and calculating Crow of Mounts Bay.

Finally I shrug. "No one will ever know about the favor if he's dead. Illi will have it done by tomorrow night and half our problems would be over with."

Atticus cuts me a look, shifting closer to me subconsciously because we've always been drawn to each other. "If we don't hold to the rules of the Twelve, we're no better than the Jackal. If favors mean nothing then the power the Wolf has fought for years to amass means nothing, and she goes back to being a poor kid from the Bay again."

My mouth tugs into a frown but, dammit, he's right about that. How many times has Lips come in and saved the day with a blood diamond she fought and killed for? Without them she's still an assassin, a killer, the smartest and most cunning girl in the room, but with no extra backup.

Only the family behind her.

It's not nothing, but twelve people against a whole city… it's not enough. Not when the other members are all recruiting to fill the void the Jackal has now left in the city and there's been such a shift in power.

"We have three candidates, and I don't want any of them dead."

Atticus sighs and rubs both of his hands over his face, shifting again until his knee touches mine. That shouldn't be such a big thing to me, considering he fucked me in a supply closet in a jealous rage, but this Atticus really is the one I've missed the most.

The Atticus who loves me.

"You really want the Ammoscato girl to survive? I thought you were playing with her."

I shrug. "She's an asset. We need more of those and less pathetic, egotistical, greedy men."

"And what if she turns out like her aunt? The Lynx was just as bad as the Bear. She just read the board wrong and ended up dead because of it."

I reach out and take his hand. "If she betrays the Wolf, she'll end up exactly like her aunt. There's something... there's something about her. My gut hasn't been wrong about this before, and the last time I had this feeling it was about Lips. Harley before that. If she wins, I'll bet that she'll be useful to us all at the very least. She's already agreed to help with the skin auctions, and we both know that's next on the Bear's agenda."

Atticus squeezes my fingers. "I offered to help him get his feet back under himself to get his garages and acid tanks back up and running, but the Feds shook him up too much. Pathetic."

I giggle. "How long does the diamond keep him breathing? You've only promised yourself, right? It's not like you can stop me from arranging something with Illi."

He pulls me into his body, finally, and rests his cheek on my head. "He handed the diamond back over in front of the Ox and the Viper. It's for his life until the Games are over with. We can't kill him, Avery."

I'm not so sure about that.

I could definitely have him taken down in a variety of different ways that wouldn't even lead back to us. The Ox, the Viper, and God himself could be suspicious, but they'd never figure it out.

My phone buzzes in my pocket, breaking the moment, and when I pull it out, it's a text from Aodhan about grabbing us both dinner. Atticus stares at the screen and I have to steel myself for whatever he has to say.

"I don't like him, Avery. He showed up out of the blue and wormed his way into your good graces. People from the Bay don't just… they don't just fall for girls like you."

I arch an eyebrow and stand up. "Your jealousy is coming through a little strong. It wasn't out of the blue; we survived the Jackal together. That sort of thing ties people together, you know that."

He stands and looks over to where Illi is waiting, watching his every move with a gun aimed at him I'm sure. "I know too much about that."

My heart stops.

"What the hell did Luca tell you?"

The moment the words leave my lips, I can see my mistake. All of the calm, strong, protective energy just seeps out of him and the cruel and stone-faced Crow is left behind. "What exactly would he know to tell me? What the hell happened in that room, Avery?"

I turn away from him, another mistake, but he was my safe

place and my strongest, most loyal ally for too long for me to face him right now.

"I'll fucking kill him. What are you doing with him if he's hurt you, Avery, you should have come to me and I—"

"He didn't hurt me. He did everything he could possibly do to die in my place, and I did what little I could to keep him alive. I don't want to talk about it and… I was afraid Luca had spoken to you about it. Please just forget I said anything."

His face doesn't soften at all, and I know he's going to leave here and go straight to Luca until he gets the answers he's looking for. I still don't know if Luca will be able to lie convincingly, but it's my own fault for panicking and giving him the idea.

"Atticus, please. If you really want us to be able to work together to survive here or for there to be a chance for us to be together someday, you need to listen to me and just… forget about it. I've done my healing from what the Jackal did to Aodhan and I. I've made my peace with it."

He doesn't say another word as he walks over to his own car, waiting until I'm back safely in the BMW with Illi before he leaves.

Aodhan's arms are tight around me and even though I can't sleep after seeing Atticus, I have no intention of moving from this bed ever again when my phone pings on my nightstand.

When I turn it onto silent each night before bed, there's a

list of contacts that I have set to still alert me if they call or text, so I know I can't ignore it. If something happened to a member of my family while I was moping and ignoring the world, I'd never forgive myself.

Mostly it's Ash seething about something that's happening on tour involving Lips, or Harley checking in on me as though he isn't getting daily updates from his cousin, so when I see the number, I startle a little, and Aodhan grunts at the movement in his sleep.

One of the rooms at the Oakridge has been booked out with a flagged guest.

A flagged guest.

It could be anyone really, but my gut drops all the same.

Elijah Blakeley. He's being taken to the third sub-floor.

Jesus H. Christ.

I sit up and hit dial on Lips' number, sliding out of the bed and scampering across the room into the bathroom. It takes three rings for her to pick up, so she was either asleep or partaking in an orgy that would scar me for life to hear any details about.

There's things a girl doesn't need to know about her brother, cousin, and Morrison.

"What's happened? Avery, are you okay?" she whispers down the line, the sounds of sheets rustling and Morrison's soft snoring coming through clearly as she moves away from the bed.

"Someone is about to assassinate Senator Blakeley. You're too far away; I'll be on a flight over to DC in an hour."

I switch the phone to speaker to start arranging everything as she mutters a curse under her breath. "How the fuck did you find that out? Jesus, I haven't even met him yet and he's already stirring shit. Is Aodhan going with you?"

"He will. Illi won't be able to come, not with Odie so far along, but I have some contacts in DC that'll come in handy. Don't worry about a thing, Lips, I have this covered."

She scoffs at me and covers the mouthpiece to speak to whoever she woke up crawling out of the bed. I'd put money on Harley.

"I can be in DC in a couple of hours. Let me come with you."

The bathroom door opens and Aodhan ducks his head in, his eyes a little bloodshot after only a couple of hours of sleep. "We've got it covered. I have family up there as well if we need it."

I smile at him. "I'll call you if I need anything, Lips, but... I promise I won't let anything happen to him. I've already got eyes on him."

I climb into the shower with Aodhan, mostly to save time, but also because he's too freaking hot for words all soaped up. It doesn't matter how many nights we fall into bed together, naked and desperate, I can't get enough of him. I know exactly how Lips felt when she told me back in senior year that she was addicted to all three of her guys.

We don't have time to fuck in the shower, no matter how

badly I want to.

I pack a small overnight bag that's still three times bigger than Aodhan's. He calls Jack to let him know where we're going and to give him the details on the next job they're supposed to be taking for the Boar at the docks.

Then he drives me to the private airstrip just outside of the city limits as though the car is on fire. There isn't a cop in the Bay who doesn't know who this Impala belongs to, and no one stops us. I'm buckled in tightly and managing the barrage of text messages from everyone at our impromptu trip.

Take all of the weapons, kid. Remember to stab first.

Tell Aodhan not to let you out of his fucking sight, Floss, Ash is losing his fucking head over this.

I'm sending backup. You shouldn't be traveling without security, Avery.

I sigh at Atticus' text and reply with a curt, *I have more than enough security waiting for me there.*

I have Senior's private jet fueled and ready for take off at all times for this exact purpose. It's something that Lips and Harley would chew me out over, because of the expense, but what is the point of being richer than God if you can't get a flight out of this city in under an hour.

We park up in the Beaumont air hanger, and the jet is waiting for us, still in perfect condition.

The pilot looks calm and respectful as he greets us onboard, and the air hostesses are both dressed appropriately with polite smiles on their faces. Neither of them attempt to flirt with

Aodhan, even when he grins and thanks them like a typical Mounty, so that also gets them points. They take the bags from Aodhan and stash them away before offering us both drinks.

I take a champagne, just to take the edge off and hopefully kickstart my brain a little, but Aodhan politely declines.

He looks sick the entire flight.

There's a fine tremble in his hand the entire time we're taking off down the runway and when the wheels lift from the tarmac, he makes a groaning noise that sounds like he's trying not to vomit all over us both.

I sip at my champagne and keep my eyes off of him, even as I slip my hand in his.

I know there's nothing worse than having people watch you while you're feeling desperately out of control like he is right now, so I give him the grace of what little privacy I can while he's gripping me like we're both drowning.

"Fuck this. We could've driven."

I smirk and pick up my phone, thumbing through the file of information Jackson has sent me. "We're on a very tight time crunch here and, given that you're a Mounty, you would have complained at my choices in accommodation along the way."

He grimaces as we hit a little turbulence and grunts, "I don't care about that shit; it's your money and I'm sure you're not worried about it running out any time soon."

I shrug and squeeze his fingers. "Stop freaking out, it's only four hours. You could have a nap."

"Fuck sleeping. If I'm gonna fall out of the sky and die, I'd like to know it's happening."

I roll my eyes at him, scrolling through my phone. "Are you going to tell me about what you and Illi found now? About the photos?"

He groans again, looking sick for a whole new reason. "One of the Viper's favorite fighters had been talking about the extra suits in the Bay. It's gotta be connected, how much weird fucking shit can be going on at once? We tracked a couple down, but one of them threw himself at Illi's knife. Just fucking impaled himself and then lay down to bleed out. It was the craziest shit I've ever seen, and the second guy charged us until I had to put him down. It was that or let him kill us, so whoever is sending them down here is picking the most suicidal, crazy fuckers he can find."

I frown at him because what the actual *fuck* is going on?

He nods. "Exactly. There's nothing really I can tell you yet, but Illi did get Jackson onto finding the footage. He didn't say a word about what they were and he was... very clear about keeping his mouth shut about anything he might see. Lips called him too, just to ram that shit home. We're going to find them, Queenie."

I nod because I believe him.

The alternative is too scary to think about.

The Ruthless

Chapter Ten

"Charlotte Gamble, the owner and manageress of the Oakridge. The woman who runs the most infamous murder-hotel in the country called you about a senator being assassinated there today and that's why we've flown our asses over here in such a hurry. Am I getting this right?" Aodhan says, his eyes on the partition between the driver and us. The town car was also one of my father's, but the driver is new.

I didn't keep any of his compliant, morally corrupt staff.

I try not to smirk like a smug bitch. "That about covers it. Problem?"

The traffic in DC is actually worse than the Bay and I'm starting to worry about not making it to Oakridge in time. There's only two blocks to go but we haven't moved for eight minutes and I'm about to scream.

"Nope, no problem. I'm just along for the ride here, Queenie. Nothing fucking better than watching you destroy everything in your path."

I grin at him, shrugging. "You might even get to help me this time around."

He huffs under his breath at me as the car *finally* moves. "I'll do what I can to stay out of your way."

The Oakridge is thirty years old but impeccably maintained, easily the most lavish old money hotel in the entire city. When the driver stops, one of the doormen dashes over to open my door for me, waiting until Aodhan slides out before retrieving our bags from the trunk.

Everyone who works here already knows who I am and where we're staying.

I slip the doorman a tip and then walk straight into the building, walking straight past the beautifully ornate double elevators and down the hall into the service elevator.

"No checking in?" Aodhan murmurs and I shake my head.

"Beaumonts don't check-in at the Oakridge. Just remember what I said; speak to no one and stay close to me."

I scan the card I always have tucked in my purse, one of the few emergency items that move around from Birkin to Birkin just in case a moment like this comes up.

Aodhan takes a half step to me until I'm pressed against him. "Like you'll be able to get rid of me, I'll be on this ass of yours until I can ride it later."

Well.

That sounds like a perfect way to finish the evening.

I smirk over my shoulder at him and then I step into the

service elevator as it opens.

There aren't any buttons, only a panel to scan your card.

"If this isn't the creepiest fucking place you've ever taken me, Queenie. Are you sure you're not dragging me down to the depths of hell?"

I shouldn't be flirting, we're heading down to the bar area which will be full to the brim of all of the biggest criminal players in the country's capital. There'll be people staying here from every corner of the world, all of them coming together to visit the famous murder-hotel that will cater to their every whim.

I take a deep breath before the doors open and then murmur quietly, "Does it matter where I'm taking you? You'll come with me, right?"

I don't need the squeeze of his hand in mine to know I'm right, he's with me no matter what. As much as I fucking loathe the Jackal and what he did to us, at least we have each other now.

There's a small ping sound and then the doors open.

The bar is teeming with people.

There isn't a set dress code down here, so it's a melting pot of evil. Bikers, suits, and gangsters, they all sit around together with drinks in their hands in a basement bar that might as well be a bomb shelter.

It's been years since I was last here and honestly, I didn't think I'd be here without Lips or Illi. The information that comes out of this place is renowned because of the strict 'no violence' ruling. There's never been a assassination down here in the thirty years that Oakridge has been operating.

Probably because of the play rooms.

Why bother getting kicked out of the club, or taken out of existence entirely, for killing here when there are purpose built murder rooms for reseravation? You don't even have to clean up after yourself, everything is covered in the fees here.

It was Senior's favorite holiday location.

So much so that he had one of the rooms here fitted out to his specific tastes and requirements, and I was sure to have that room destroyed the second Senior was wheeled into the morgue. It was much easier to sleep knowing that, slowly but surely, I would wipe any remnants of that man's existence from this Earth.

The only things left will be Ash and I.

I won't rest until I'm sure of that.

Aodhan finally looks more comfortable now that we're back in disreputable company. He leans down to murmur into my ear, "Fuck. There's a few of the bikers from your wall in here. All of them are Demons, they don't know you're looking for them, do they?"

I turn into his chest, my head tilted back so we look like besotted lovers and not scheming criminals. "They're unaware. I'm not here for them tonight anyway. If you can catch anything they're talking about though, that would be helpful."

He nods and drops a kiss onto my lips, softly enough that my lipstick doesn't smudge.

He's too perfect for me sometimes.

I don't deserve it.

I walk in slowly, looking for the real reason we're here and finding her at the bar with a cocktail in her hands, the all-black pantsuit she's in looking amazing on her curves.

I'm almost jealous.

Charlotte meets my eyes from across the room and jerks her head at me. I wouldn't take that sort of summoning from anyone normally, but she's been too good at taking care of my business for me to split hairs right now.

The moment we get to her, she leans in close to my ear to murmur, "He's already here, I was about to go deal with the whole situation without you."

Aodhan shifts so his body is covering us both a little better as I reply, "There's limits to how fast I can get across the country. Which room are they in? I need him out of here now."

She smiles and leads the way, cutting through the room like she owns the place because, well, she does. Every person who frequents the bar knows it too, moving out of her way like her ass is on fire and they don't want to get burned.

Nothing better than a woman getting the respect she deserves, her hands dripping with the blood she shed to get it.

"A bullet in the head or an interrogation?"

I glance over my shoulder at Aodhan but he's focused entirely on protecting me from any wandering hands. "An interrogation. The senator needs to be released first, but I need to know who is trying to get rid of him."

Charlotte smirks as we step into the elevator, pulling out a tablet to check the security cameras. "Don't like people touching your toys? I have other senators you can have, you know, if you lose this one."

I shrug, feigning indifference, because no one needs to know how much I'm willing to do to keep Lips' siblings alive until we know if we're keeping them or not. "I'm rather attached and, besides, it's the principle of it. No one breaks my *toys* except me."

Charlotte giggles and we step out onto the sub-floor. I wait until she's not looking before I take a breath, just enough air in to stay calm and not let the lingering memories of this place take over me. I'm fine, there's no one here who could ever hurt me, and the ghosts of the men I saw die here are most certainly in hell and not lurking around the corner waiting to finally take a piece out of me.

There's only four rooms on each sub-floor and only three sub-floors to the hotel. Each was purposely built for easy cleanup and they have a wide variety of weapons, props, and tools to suit any purpose. The walls are thick enough that even the loudest of screams can't be heard outside of the room itself, and the doors can only be opened with the cards you pick up from the reception.

Unless you're Charlotte and have a master key.

The door opens with a quiet beeping noise and she pushes straight in, her heels clicking on the concrete flooring as loud as gunshots in the silence of the room.

Aodhan follows me in without hesitation.

Blakeley is chained to a chair in the center of the room, a bag over his head and by the muffled grunts I'd guess he's got a gag in his mouth too. The suit he's wearing is a little disheveled, some blood down the front that says his nose is probably broken, and his shoes are missing.

We were a little too close.

"This room is occupied, cunt! Go have your fucking threesome somewhere else."

I glance over at the biker piece of shit talking, and he's utterly forgettable. The type of guy that blends into a crowd of other rough bikers. He's ripped but not in a bulky way, and the cut over his shoulders reads proudly 'Chaos Demons'.

Grimm sent him here to kill his bastard son.

"Mister Jones, I'm sorry to say you've checked into my hotel and there are guidelines here. You've broken one of the strictest rules in place, so I'm going to have to deal with this issue accordingly," Charlotte says in her best customer service voice. Honestly, it gives me chills.

The biker's lip curls as he turns, but Charlotte lifts a hand and nails him in the chest with a taser gun, taking him down to the ground with ease.

She steps forward and presses her foot over his throat, her mouth a red slash of smirking wrath across her face. "I'm not really a fan of being called a cunt."

Aodhan steps around me to go get the biker restrained before he comes to, nodding his head respectfully at Charlotte. She looks at him with interest but the same type she gives every newcomer to the Oakridge, so I don't feel the need to stab her in the kidneys which is good.

I'm wearing white after all.

I go to get Blakeley up and out of this room before he sees anything else that's too revealing. I somehow need to convince him not to send the Feds down here and make a headache for us all to have to clean up, and his reputation as a law-abiding citizen and hard-ass has me concerned about how this is all going to play out—but he's alive.

That's the important thing.

It takes me a second to get the restraints holding him to the floor untied and then I firmly guide him to stand up, walking over to the door and pressing the release button to get us out of there.

"Queenie, if you leave this room without me you will not like the consequences," Aodhan calls out, and I huff at him, but I do pause long enough for him to finish getting the biker trussed up.

Charlotte smirks at me over his shoulder, and I roll my eyes at her.

"Don't deal with the issue until after I'm back. I have some questions for him," I say as Aodhan grabs Blakeley's arm and Charlotte nods, slowly running her hands over the rack of weapons that were intended for the senator.

I'm sure there'll be some pieces missing from the biker before we get back.

I'm also sure I don't give a fuck.

We walk Blakeley over to the elevator and step in together, my card getting us back up to the main floor. I get out my phone and arrange for my town car to circle back to pick the senator up and take him back to his offices.

I direct Aodhan out to the back of the hotel to where the valet parking is, away from prying eyes and with less security cameras for me to have to deal with, and it's only when we have Blakeley sitting in the car that I finally speak to him.

"Senator, forgive me for meeting you under such difficult circumstances, but please rest assured that my driver will see you home. You may want to triple your security for the time being, just until we're able to find out who wants you dead. The Wolf of Mounts Bay sends her regards."

His spine snaps straight, but I shut the car door before he can start swearing and struggling against the bonds and gag.

We can argue about it later.

"He didn't seem… happy to see you. Does he even know he's in your pocket?" Aodhan says as we walk back over to the service elevator.

I flick the card around and scan the other end of it to get

us to the correct floor, Aodhan's eyes taking the action in. "He's not in my pocket and… he's not going to be. I need him alive for other reasons."

He nods slowly and takes my hand. "Secret reason, got it."

He's too good for me.

As suspected, when we get back to the room, the biker is bleeding everywhere, and Charlotte has her jacket off and her crisp black button-down sleeves rolled back to her elbows.

"He doesn't have that much to say. He wanted the senator's agenda to disappear."

I sigh and step over a large piece of flesh on the floor so I can get a good look at his face as I question him. I try not to think about all of the holes in him now.

"Was it Grimm himself who asked you to kill him or some other higher-up?"

"Councilman. The higher-ups in the MC are the councilmen," Aodhan says, leaning against the wall where he can still be within arm's reach.

The biker opens his mouth and blood comes pouring out, flecks of it spitting out at me as he speaks. "Grimm wanted him dead. Blocking the imports will shut half our shit down. He's a fucking do-gooder, those types don't last in politics. You'll never fucking turn the cunt, every man and his dog have tried."

Jesus.

It still doesn't help me hazard a guess over whether or not the president of the Chaos Demons knows that Blakeley is his biological son, and that's the real question I need answered tonight.

I can't ask it with Aodhan and Charlotte around, and chances are this guy wouldn't know anyway. Better to cut my losses and just be done with this conversation.

We got Blakeley out alive.

I'll speak with him tomorrow.

"We're done here," I say, straightening up and nodding at Charlotte. She smirks and pulls out a huge knife, too big for how small her hand is, and I turn away before I have to see it.

I also take three very large steps away so my outfit isn't completely ruined. Aodhan watches the whole thing but I only listen as Charlotte slits his throat, the biker gagging and gasping and choking through the wound until he bleeds out. It's a pretty quick process, but I feel like it drags on forever.

Disgusting.

I need a long, hot, sterile shower.

"I'll meet you down in the private bar, Beaumont. We can share a drink before you head up for the night. I know you've had a long day," Charlotte says, and I nod.

"I'll call for the cleaning crew, just to speed things along."

Aodhan holds my hand the entire way down in the elevator, only dropping it when they open back up into the bar. He knows how rattled the blood-soaked parts of this life can make me. I couldn't care less about the death but all of that DNA just spurting out everywhere around me?

It's enough to have me screaming and running the hell out of this place.

The bartender at the end of the bar lets us through and into the private rooms without a word, nodding at me respectfully and keeping her eyes away from us both. It reminds me of how everyone in the Bay treats Lips and has me smiling a little.

I wait until we're seated in the plush lounge before I update her on how the evening has gone. She doesn't have any questions about her brother, only about my safety, but I tell her I'll have more to say about him tomorrow anyway.

I don't have very high hopes.

"The enforcer of the Chaos Demons is here. They're going to notice their brother is missing and come after the hotel," Aodhan murmurs, and I shrug.

"The Oakridge has very strict rules. If they ask about him, Charlotte will inform them that he broke a rule and paid the price. They can get angry about it but, honestly, this place is more valuable to them than some underling. I can't imagine they'd wage war over *Jones*."

Aodhan nods and then straightens slightly as Charlotte walks in, two drinks in her hands. "Sorry! I only know what Beaumont drinks so you'll have to forgive me, Stag."

He shrugs and says, "I'm keeping my head about me tonight."

She smirks at him and takes a seat, handing me a glass and then clinking it with her own. "It's been too long! You should visit more often."

I roll my eyes at her. "You've been too busy to even notice how long it's been, Gamble. The revenues have tripled here since you took over. A lot of money in murder."

She grins at me again, all teeth and smugness, sipping away at her drink. Aodhan stares at her for a moment too long, like he's trying to memorize every little part of her face, and I know he has no idea of how he should be acting in this situation.

"So why are you protecting the senator? He's well-known around here, the type that gets up everyone's asses and has the whole club bitching about him."

I shrug and take a sip from the glass. Margaritas are my preferred drink of choice but the gin and tonic she mixed for me is top shelf and smooth enough. "He's on my protection list for now."

Charlotte sighs and smirks at me. "And that's all you'll tell me? Classic Beaumont."

I take another sip as Aodhan's eyes bounce between us before focusing once again on Charlotte. "This is an... interesting business. Did you inherit it or build it?"

She smiles at him in a way I don't at all like and his face tightens up a little around the edges in response, clearly not happy with her interest. "I inherited my half of the business from my father. He built it with an old friend. The two of them designed each and every one of the rooms here, they came up with all of the rules and vetted each and every member. It's not for everyone but I wasn't made for living a clean life. I always wanted blood."

He gives her a curt nod. "And the other owner? Do you get along with them?"

Charlotte grins and flicks her eyes over to me. "Avery and I go way back. There's no one else I would want to share Oakridge with."

I ignore the flash of Aodhan's eyes as they snap back to me. "Technically, you share it with Ash and I now that Senior is gone, but he wants the place burned to the ground. I'm a little more business savvy than that."

Charlotte smirks. "And thank God for that. I'd hate to have to go straight if this place shut down. Can you imagine me bartending for real? No fucking thanks!"

I refuse a second drink, even though she tries to insist, because running on zero sleep is finally starting to hit me now that I know Blakeley is home safe and the adrenaline has seeped out of me.

We make our excuses and head back up to the main floor to the other set of elevators to get to our room. Dozens of people are walking around, completely unaware of what is taking place under their feet.

As we stand at the main elevator, waiting, Aodhan takes my hand in his again and brings my knuckles up to his lips. "Why does Ash want this place destroyed? He never seemed squeamish to me and it obviously has its uses."

I shrug. "He's not but I almost died down there once… and it's the first place Ash ever killed someone. Not that he cares about that sort of thing, but his first blood wasn't exactly… I was attacked in there and he found me. He killed the man who did it, but now he's tied the whole thing up into this place being too dangerous for me. He's not exactly… rational sometimes when it comes to my safety."

Aodhan nods and smirks at me. "So you've told him exactly nothing about what's been happening since he left the Bay?"

I smile back at him. "I've told him plenty! I'm sure he's thrilled to hear about all of the baking I've been doing while absolutely nothing dangerous is happening in the Bay. Didn't you hear, it's become the safest city in the country? A miracle really."

He chuckles at me, tucking me in closer to his body. "How much do you think Lips is telling him? What about Harley? I doubt he's taking all of this well."

The elevator bell chimes and we step in together, scanning the card to head up to the penthouse suite. "Harley is less… single-minded about it. He knows that Lips has trained me well and I can kill if I have to. I don't think he knows everything, but I wouldn't be surprised if Lips leaned on him a little more with this stuff."

I also wouldn't be surprised if she tells him nothing.

She's a smart girl.

Chapter Eleven

I wake up hours before my alarm goes off in a cold sweat, the old memories of this hotel clinging to me. I decided a long time ago I wouldn't be afraid of the sub-levels, even before Senior was removed from the picture, but something about talking to Aodhan seems to have dredged it all back up.

The last thing in my mind before my eyes open, my entire body shaking like a freaking leaf and my heart trying to beat out of my chest, is Ash's face covered in blood and the panicked fury in his eyes when he'd finished killing the man that lured me out of my room to kill me.

I've never been so naive again.

That girl died here in the hotel and the jaded, ruthless version of myself took over. A piece of Ash died here too, the boy who didn't want to ever kill anyone because he didn't want to become like our father.

Now he just refuses to kill women, even the ones who deserve it.

I lie here, naked, and listen to Aodhan breathe. I'm jealous of how deeply he sleeps. Even if I do wake him up, he can still always roll over and go back to sleep which is a super power I've never had. My brain always starts running a mile a minute, running through everything possible that I can think about until I go insane and get up for a coffee so that I can start to plan a riot to make myself feel better.

I can't really do that here at Oakridge, so instead I slide down Aodhan's body and wake him up with a blowjob.

I know the moment he wakes up because his hips jerk up, and he fists my hair to push me further down his length. He always manages to walk that line between handling me like I'm precious to him without coddling me, and there's nothing quite like the taste of him on my tongue.

He pulls me off of him before he comes, dragging me up his body until I'm straddling him, his dick sinking in deep, and that fist in my hair pulling me down to kiss him.

I think I'm in love with him.

"Fuck, Queenie, I could wake up every morning with that perfect pussy on me and it still wouldn't be enough. Fuck, move, I need you to come on me. I need to feel you come all over my dick before I blow."

With one hand in my hair and the other on my clit, I can't help but follow his every direction, swinging my hips and grinding myself against him until I come, his head dropping back against the pillows as he watches me fall apart.

Then his hands move to my hips to hold me still as he fucks me through the aftershocks, coming with a groan loud enough to wake the dead.

I collapse onto the bed next to him, panting and shaking, and he kisses me again, long and deep until I find myself gearing up for round two.

Then my alarm starts screaming, and the outside world once again ruins everything. I have a meeting with a senator that I can't miss, and we need to get back to Mounts Bay before the first round of the Game starts.

We shower together and then I get ready, choosing an old money looking skirt and blazer combo in a very pale cream color. Only I would really be able to tell that it's not true white and when I bought it, Lips had rolled her eyes at my critique of the color.

Only you would give a fuck about that level of color theory, Aves.

I put Aodhan in a suit to go meet with Senator Blakeley.

He's not exactly thrilled about it, but he takes it better than Illi ever did so I'll call it a win. I sneak a photo of us both in the elevator mirror on the way out and send it to Lips.

I swear you could talk the Devil himself into a penguin suit if you tried. Aodhan looks great, tell him to stab first.

I huff at her because that's ridiculous. *I've met the Devil, he wasn't impressed by me.*

Lips had been completely unsure about us going to this meeting, but I convinced her it's the right thing to do. We can't leave DC without actually speaking with Senator Elijah Blakeley, the oldest and most suppressed Graves sibling. Helping him at Oakridge hadn't given me any idea of who he is as a man, the stuff that Jackson's file can't tell me, and I need those little insights to plan out what we're going to do about him.

The drive over to the Senate office buildings takes almost an hour thanks to the traffic, and Aodhan can barely sit still in his seat.

"This thing looks ridiculous; I can't believe you have fucking suits in my size. Did you measure me while I slept?"

I roll my eyes at his disgruntled tone but keep my eyes on my screen. "I'll never tell you my methods, but you do look amazing. Lips even said so and she's as Mounty as you are."

He huffs at me and leans down to whisper in my ear, "When all of this bullshit is over with, and your little stalker is rotting in a ditch somewhere, I'm taking you to a party at the docks, and you can dress up in the shit the girls down there do. See how you like the tables being turned on you."

I've seen a few of the outfits Lips has worn to the parties over the years, and it doesn't sound like the worst idea ever. I mean, it's not at all my style and my ass is nowhere near as great as hers is in booty shorts, but it could be fun for a night out.

"Deal, but if you try to eat me out in public, I will claw your eyeballs out. I do have some lines, you know."

He frowns at me and nods, but I guess that's a family joke he's not in on yet, and I still don't have the stomach to explain it to him.

The Senate office buildings are overrun with security, clearly the kidnapping and near murder has upped the alert level appropriately. The security checks themselves are invasive and off-putting to get into the building. It's the first time I've left my weapons behind since Illi gave them to me and without the Kevlar, I'm finally feeling like myself again, like the girl who doesn't need weapons because my scathing wit and list of contacts is more than enough.

I should just leave the weapons to Lips.

I'm just about ready to have her home again.

Once we make our way through the building and into Blakeley's office, the waiting room is very stereotypical 'all-American senator'-chic. Aodhan looks around at everything like he's uncomfortable to be here, and it's a strange look on him. I'm used to the self-assured man that he is in the Bay; even when faced with the crime lords of the Twelve, he's always been confident in himself and his ability to deal with whatever is thrown at him.

There's something about the fact that we're dealing with a member of the Senate that has him worried.

I feel right at home.

I try not to fuss with my outfit, because I look perfect, and I slip my hand into Aodhan's to try to offer him some reassurance. There's nothing worse than feeling completely out of your depth, and he's only really here to watch out for me and keep me company.

We wait for ten minutes, and Blakeley's personal assistant keeps looking over at us like we're a threat to the building. I find myself wondering about how much Blakeley has told those in his staff and his inner circles about what happened to him last night.

I'm trying not to pick up my phone and obsessively scroll when the door opens and a very well-dressed woman walks in with two small children. She's very clearly a nanny, I was raised by them after my mother's death and can spot them from a mile away, but she's very open and affectionate with them both. The toddler in her arms is a boy, giggling and babbling to her, and the little girl at her feet grips her hand tightly with a bright grin.

All of the air in my lungs leaks out of me.

The girl giggles at something Blakeley's personal assistant says, and Aodhan curses under his breath, focused on the look of shock on my face, but I ignore him, entirely focused on Lips' niece.

Grimm Graves really did pass his genes on well.

"You wanna tell me who the fuck we're really here to see before I look like a dumbass in there? You look like you've seen a ghost," Aodhan murmurs, but there isn't any real anger in his voice, just concern.

I run a calm hand down the luxurious softness of my cashmere and silk skirt. "You're here because I trust you and, more importantly, *Lips* trusts you. There's some... finer details of her parentage that we can discuss later, but I can't speak about them unless we're absolutely sure that no one can overhear."

He freezes, and I think for a second that he's actually pissed off at me for not answering him, but when I glance over at him, his eyes are on the door, finally noticing the girl.

There's no mistaking the relation.

"Holy fucking shit."

The door to Blakeley's office opens and he steps out, missing us completely because he only has eyes for his kids. Big brownie points in his favor there, because there's no mistaking the love between the three of them as he kisses each of the kids on their heads and listens to their excitement to see him.

"I have one meeting left and then I'll take you out to lunch, Kennedy. Giorgio has reserved us a table; he's going to make your favorite. Be good for Sue. Carter, you too, be a good boy, and I'll see you all over there shortly."

Kennedy and Carter Blakeley.

Fitting.

I knew they existed but seeing them here, seeing this little interaction, it's changing something. It's changed the way I'm going to go about this, how hard I'm going to push, and what I'm going to say because… because in our family there are very few good fathers. Harley had one who was murdered for it, and Illi is going to be the best father.

I guess I hold men to that standard.

Their loyalty, their ability to love and protect and covet, and how they treat children. Maybe that's my line in the sand.

Blakeley turns back to his office and finally spots us sitting there, his back stiffening, a sure sign that he knows at least a little about who he's meeting with.

"Miss Beaumont, sorry to keep you waiting. Please join me."

Oh, he definitely knows who I am and doesn't like me.

I nod with a curt smile and then murmur to Aodhan, "Wait here."

He gives me a look, but I can't afford to argue with him right now so I tack on, "I'll tell you everything when we get back to the Bay. I promise."

I step into the office, shutting the door behind myself, and Blakeley walks around to the other side of the desk, unbuttoning his jacket before taking a seat. It's like watching Lips move, or like Nate is sitting there in a suit, and a chill runs down my spine.

How the hell does this man have such strong genes?

"I'd rather not beat around the bush here, Miss Beaumont. Are you here to threaten me?"

I take a seat, impressed as hell at this man. "Not at all. I'm here to offer my assistance. I'm very open to siding with you on your upcoming projects."

His eyes flick to the door and then back to me. "And what exactly would the daughter of Joseph Beaumont be able to offer me that isn't blood money? I've kept my hands clean this long; I'll make it on my own without sullying myself."

Okay, that stings a little but I'll take it. At least this is all coming from a moral high ground and not just a superiority complex. Thank God Aodhan isn't in here with us. "How did you get your medical file sealed, Blakeley? That wasn't done *cleanly*."

He's good, I'll give him that, but I'm watching him too closely to miss the way he stops breathing. "Medical files are confidential—"

I interrupt him, "They are but only a sealed file would be able to withstand the types of searching I'm talking about. It took the Coyote of Mounts Bay himself to find out what I needed to know."

If I wasn't already sure the room was clean, I am the moment he recovers enough to answer me. "Whatever that psychotic, rapist fuck Graves wants, I'll never give to him. I'll burn his business to the ground before I fall into line behind that man so you can leave, Miss Beaumont. Leave and tell him that."

Huh.

I wasn't expecting him to know much about his father. "Is that why he's sending men to have you killed? It was a close call; you're lucky I had eyes on you and got you out of there."

His mouth turns down at the corners, as close to a sneer as I've seen on him so far. "I'll admit my security obviously failed. It won't next time. Please see yourself out, Miss Beaumont, I have no intention of ever selling my soul and certainly not to someone like you."

Again, ouch. He's really trying his hardest to get me to hate him, but I'm in this for the long game. I'm in this for Lips and for those little children out there who have a good father and need him to stay alive. "You have other siblings."

Blakely shrugs. "I don't care about biker brats, I just want to be left alone."

It's a gamble but one that I'd warned Lips I might have to take. "And the others? Do you care about the bastard children Grimm spawned all over the country? At what point would you be tempted into joining the family?"

His lip curls. "I have a family. I have parents, I have a wife, I have children—I don't need little lost siblings who have their hands out for money."

Right.

Clearly this relationship building exercise is going to take action not words. That's perfectly fine, I have enough eyes on Blakeley now that we can just swoop in to save him again and again until he falls into line.

I really don't want to own him.

I just want him breathing.

I stand up, taking a card out of my pocket and sliding it across the table. "That's my contact number. I don't want you in my pocket, Senator Blakeley, I want to keep you out of anyone else's. You might not care about your lost siblings, but I do, and I'll do anything to keep them safe. Keeping you out of danger means you can't be held over anyone else's head and that's all I'm trying to do here."

Blakeley's hands tighten into fists, his lip curling, and finally he looks a little bit more like a Graves. Not a lot, but there's that fire to him that I'm so used to seeing in Lips and Nate.

Colt has it too.

He leans back in his chair and slowly the fire slips away until he looks more like the senator he's supposed to be in this room. I'm expecting a brush off dismissal but his words surprise me. "I will destroy that man and everything he's built. If you get in my way then I'll destroy you too. You're everything that's wrong with this country, Miss Beaumont, and I won't stop until you and all of the other degenerate vultures peddling drugs, guns, and women are locked up on death row where you belong."

Right.

I don't like being threatened at the best of times, but the air of superiority is just a little too much for me today. Especially since I just saved his ass at Oakridge.

Time to leave before I have to explain to Lips that I murdered her brother but he totally deserved it.

I stand and walk to the door, opening it before pausing again. I can't leave without knocking him down, just a little.

"You were very lucky, you know. Whatever sad little story you tell yourself about your start in life… you were the luckiest of the bunch. Two loving parents at home? I'm guessing they fed you, put a roof over your head, kissed your booboos, and told you how special you were? Sounds lovely. No one else got that. Not a single one of your siblings, and the things your sisters have survived? Unspeakable. I'm here to keep you out of Grimm's hands; you could show just a little more respect."

I open the door and Aodhan is still standing there waiting, his face setting like concrete the second he sees how pissed I am. I just want to get the hell out of here and away from that pretentious asshole, the type I grew up with and fucking *loathed*.

Blakeley calls out to me, "Why? Why bother coming here if you didn't want to blackmail me or use the power I hold?"

I turn back to stare at him, Aodhan's hand sliding into mine as he holds the door open for me. I shrug at him.

"No one touches the Wolf... or her blood."

The Ruthless

Chapter Twelve

The warehouse is on the northern city limit in an industrial area I've never been before. The entire area is teeming with the Crow's men, all of them scowling and checking people in without any of the posturing bullshit of the Jackal.

It makes for a pleasant change.

Illi parks us with the rest of the Twelve cars, between the Impala and a very new Bentley, and then we step out into the warm Bay night. It's too quiet here. The stillness of the night seems unsettling when you know what it is that we're here to do. Forty-eight nominees will come here tonight and only twenty-four will leave.

It's the first big cull.

There's two more to come and then the real fun begins.

Lucy is waiting for us at the door, leaning against the exterior wall with a cigarette hanging out of her mouth, and I startle at the hungry look in Illi's eyes until I realize he's focused entirely on the smoke curling out of her mouth.

When I giggle at him, he gives me a dark look. "I promised Odie I'd quit before the baby gets here. It's never been so fucking hard to be a man of my word to her."

I shrug at him with a smile. "I'll send you some patches, we got Morrison clean with them after his last self-destruct tour. I couldn't stand the smell of it so Ash made him quit."

He shakes his head at me with a chuckle, jerking his head at Lucy to follow us into the warehouse. He's cold and aloof with her but there's definitely the beginnings of respect there, because there's no way he could watch her take out someone responsible for trafficking women and girls without his opinion of her changing.

She could still die tonight though, so we can't get too attached.

As we walk in, I start assessing everything because that's what I do. The smell of blood is already strong in the air, and I have to choke back the bile that creeps up my throat. It's louder in here than it is outside, thanks to all the bodies, but nowhere near what I expected. There's a reverent sort of hush over the crowd, like this is something holy to them all.

I guess it is.

Lucy is wearing clothes that I can't imagine will help her stay alive. Skintight jeans just seem like a bad idea to me, and a leather jacket? Isn't that going to restrict her arms if she needs to hit someone?

I mention this to Illi, and he scoffs at me. "She's dressed like a Mounty; she's fine. What the fuck do you think I'm wearing when I head out for the night?"

"Well, not skinny jeans for Christ's sake! We need her to win."

Illi shrugs and glances around. "We don't though, not really. When it comes down to it, our skin isn't in this game at all, pun intended. It would be different if you had've put yourself in."

Shit.

I didn't realize Aodhan had told him about that, and Illi gives me a look like he's taking up Ash's spot as my brother and wants to kill me for even thinking about it.

I give him nothing but ice back. "I would've won if I wanted to. I decided to find a different crown to wear."

He huffs at me and ignores the jeering and yelling starting up from the crowd as two competitors walk into the makeshift ring taped out in the center of the room. "And I would've waded in there after you to kill any man that dared to throw you around. No one touches the Wolf or her fucking family, kid."

I duck my head to hide a smile and he nudges me gently, the closest he can get to giving me a hug in this snake-pit of a room. Lucy watches us both carefully but doesn't say a word, just follows us through the crowd as it parts for us until we stop to stand with Aodhan and Jack. Jackson is a few feet away, standing with Atticus, Luca, and a handful of the Crow's men.

He waves at me like an idiot and then cackles at the look I give him.

"Wanna put money on the fights? It's gonna be a long and boring night if we don't," Illi says, cracking his neck as he looks around the room.

He's not wrong. We have twenty-four fights to get through, and Lucy's is the last.

There's only really three fights I care about tonight, and I find myself watching Jack as he watches the fight. He looks good, dressed to fight and not nervous at all. There also isn't an air of desperation around him, which was a real concern for me.

When I told Harley he was going into the Game, he'd sighed and said, "So he's decided to die then? How's Aodhan taking the news?"

I thought he was just doubting his cousin's ability to fight but then when I'd spoken to Lips, she'd told me about their conversation with Aodhan last Christmas and the delicate state of Jack's mental health.

I don't blame him… but I also don't want to lose him.

"The fighting is that way, Queenie," Aodhan murmurs in my ear, careful not to be too close to me with this many eyes on us, but there's nothing about his stance that isn't protective and coveting.

I lean into him. "I'd rather stick pins in my eyes than watch this shit all night."

There's a loud crack and then a roar from the crowd. The fight is over and the first casualty of the Game is out. Two men in suits walk over and then drag the dead body out, tubs of acid already waiting to clean up the evidence. The victor, one of the Bear's men, whoops and roars joyfully as he leaves the circle even as blood streams down his face from the cuts and broken nose.

Atticus only waits long enough for the circle to be clear and then he calls out the next names.

It goes on for hours.

When Luca gets called, he removes his jacket and rolls up the sleeves on his shirt, looking far too dressed up compared to the shirtless, manic guy he's been paired with. Their fight is the shortest so far and in less than a minute, Luca is walking back out of the ring without a mark on him, only a single missing button on his shirt to show he'd even fought.

No one cheers for him, they all just stare at him in fear because there's no chance any of the brawlers and brute force fighters we've seen so far could win against his technique.

Relief pours through me.

I might not be able to stand looking at him right now, but I also don't want him dead. I want him alive and very far away from me until I've managed to fully process and unpack everything that happened with the Jackal. He's borne the brunt of my trauma, but I'm also very sure he can handle it.

Even if it does get him threatened by Aodhan and Illi every now and then.

"Let's fucking hope Jack and Lucy don't get paired with him anytime soon because neither of them stand a chance," Illi leans down to murmur, and I nod.

There's nothing I can do to change the pairing system. I've already tried and failed, but I do have a couple of options up my sleeve if that happens.

The problem is still the fact that we have three people and only two seats.

Lucy scoffs and kicks her boot against the concrete floor. Illi raises an eyebrow at her and drawls, "You got something to say?"

She shrugs and snarks back, "Nothing better than being underestimated."

She's being sarcastic, but it rings true deep in my chest because wasn't that how the entire legend of the infamous Wolf of Mounts Bay started? Every person in her life underestimated what she could do, how far she'd go, and what she could survive.

Until she was the last one standing.

Illi looks like he's going to chew her out just because he's bored and she's an easy target, so I cut in, "You should be watching and taking notes. You're going to face these men in some way or another in the following rounds, and the best way to survive is to know what to expect."

She shrugs and looks around at the group of bleeding and bruised men who've won so far. "I already know everything I need to about them. All men are the same."

While I can't argue with her because my own opinion of men is pretty similar, she's taking a huge risk by thinking that way in this situation. Luca just proved that not all men are walking into this fight with the same capacity.

Some are already walking in as honed killers, not just street-trained Mounties with a violent history.

When Jack's name is called, I want to throw up all over again, but I force myself to watch the entire fight. I hate it and even at two minutes it takes too freaking long, but Jack snaps the other guy's neck the minute he takes him to the ground.

It's impressive.

"Stop looking so surprised; it's a little insulting," Aodhan murmurs, and I scoff at him, rolling my eyes.

"I've never seen him fight, how is it insulting to be impressed? It's good to know I don't have to be worried here."

Lucy watches us both a little too closely, her eyes dragging over all of the parts of Aodhan that are turned into me like my body is a magnet. I don't care if the entire world knows we're together, but there's nothing I hate more than that sort of casual assessment.

As if her judgement matters to me.

Finally she looks away and says in a clear tone, loud enough for anyone around us to overhear, "If he's put in the ring with me, I'll kill him. Without question, so prepare yourself for that inevitability."

Illi huffs at her and says back, "That's the entire fucking point of the Game. Let's see you get through the first round and then you can talk your shit up."

Atticus looks over at us, Illi's raised voice grabbing his attention away from the ring, and our eyes meet. Nothing about his stance changes, not his facial expression or the cold steel of his eyes, but it's as though the gaping chasm between us has slowly filled in and now we're only steps away from each other again.

Waiting for one of us to make a move.

He gives me a curt but respectful nod, the same he would give any other member or representative. I give him the same back and then look away quickly when Luca glances over as well.

Atticus will know something is going on, but I can't fake it tonight. Not after this many fights and deaths and bodies already starting to dissolve into *goo* just a few feet away from me.

Stop thinking about it, Avery, just focus on the job.

Finally, freaking *finally*, Lucy's name gets called out.

The jeering and catcalling is so loud in the enclosed space and half of what's being said is disgusting male bullshit. They're all running on the highs of fight or flight, and there's nothing they want more than to see this blond curvy woman get destroyed in the ring.

"Fucking typical rapist bullshit," Illi murmurs, and he inches closer to me as the yelling reaches a fever pitch. The utter bullshit they're yelling out is explicit but not at all original.

One way or another they all want her broken into pieces for their enjoyment.

Aodhan can't help but look disgusted, staring around at everyone like he's taking notes of who to keep the fuck away from me and all of his many female cousins.

I admit I'm doing the same.

The Bear's men are all in on the action and half of the Viper's men. None of the bikers are joining in, but they're all murmuring amongst themselves so really they could be saying anything.

I meet Harbin's eyes across the room and he nods at me, just the slightest incline of his head. Roxas is nowhere to be seen and I'd put money on him being at Illi's place with Odie, one of the very few people the Butcher trusts with his pregnant wife.

"Did you call Harbin in for backup or did they follow the Boar along for the ride?" I murmur to Illi as Lucy strips out of her jacket and steps into the ring.

She holds out her arms to Atticus and does a slow turn, showing she doesn't have any weapons, and with how tight her clothes are, he barely looks at her before nodding and waving her into the ring.

Her opponent is three times the size of her.

I wouldn't have called her petite but, against the giant wall of muscle, she almost looks like a child. The Viper had chosen the details of this round and chosen who faced off against each other, and I'm sure he's overjoyed at how much screaming is happening at the final pairing of his choice.

"Did you put money on Lucy? You might make a killing

here," I say, and Illi gives me a lopsided grin.

"Of course. The odds were like a thousand to one, so we're gonna walk outta here loaded."

I huff because I'm worried we're about to lose our sponsor and ally against the skin markets and then I force my eyes back into the ring. No matter what happens, I'm going to watch it all.

I'm the reason she's in there; it's my responsibility to bear witness.

"I'm gonna break every fucking bone in your body and then fuck you raw, slut."

I really, really don't want to be forced to witness that, so Lucy better come through with these skills she was so smug about. Aodhan clearly doesn't think she has it in her because he shifts a little more in front of me and mutters to Illi, "Get her the hell outta here if this goes south; I don't give a fuck about keeping up appearances."

Illi meets his eye with a nod and then glances over at Atticus who is also looking over at me like I'm a ticking bomb about to go off.

The guy, Travis, lunges at Lucy and tries to grab her, lurching forward as she easily ducks out of his reach and rushes behind him, the heel of her boot slamming into the back of his knee. He stumbles a little but keeps his feet, spinning around on the spot to go at her again.

It's game over if he gets ahold of her but without a weapon, I'm not sure how she's going to get through this.

Jackson moves over to stand with us, wincing as Travis finally gets a hit in and Lucy is knocked to the ground. Her head snaps back, and he dives on her as the crowd goes mental.

Illi shifts in front of me as well, Jack shifting back until I'm completely covered by them all in case the crowd forms a fucking riot over the bloodbath that's about to start in front of us.

I was hoping for a little more than this from Lucy, disappointment curling in my gut.

Travis gets her legs split open and sinks further down onto her, propping himself up onto one hand and lifting the other hand ready to beat the life out of her just like he said he would.

One of her hands shoots up to grab him by the throat.

There's no way she has the strength to actually choke him out in this position, and he roars out a laugh, all mocking as she lifts her other hand up to his throat as well. I desperately want to look away, but I force my eyes to stay on her.

She taps her fingers and thumb together, the silver jewelry making a little clinking noise and then suddenly it's not a weirdly intricate piece of silver. It's a claw... it's a weapon.

She can't move much except her hand but the moment she sinks the claws into his throat, Travis rears back and effectively rips his own throat out with the force.

The blood pours out of his neck in the most horrifying way, his heart pumping it out as if his neck is a hose, just gushing out until Lucy is absolutely covered in it.

"I fucking love that kid. Can we adopt her?" Jackson

mumbles to me while I try not to vomit all over his shoes.

There's a stunned silence from the entire crowd, no one knowing what the hell to say because… well, we were all pretty sure she was going to be raped and murdered right there in front of us and now she's grinning like a lunatic, the whites of her teeth stark against her blood-soaked body.

Atticus steps into the taped off ring and says, "It's over. Lucy moves onto the next round."

The Bear snarls from across the room, "She fucking cheated! No fucking weapons allowed!"

Atticus stares over at him, the room falling deathly silent. "Travis is dead. Lucy moves on. Now leave before anyone else ends up in an acid bath."

The room is quiet, no one celebrating or happy about the girl winning. I'm sure there'll be a bitch fit over her jewelry, but they're saving it for when the Crow's men aren't crawling all around them all. It doesn't matter to me.

I can deal with that aftermath.

We stay put, waiting for the crowd to disperse so we're not having to fight our way through all of the disgusting bodies to get out of here. Aodhan's hand slips into mine, squeezing gently as we watch Lucy walk over to us as if she isn't covered in blood.

It drips down her face, and she smiles like it's *nothing*. "Not the first time I've ripped a throat out in my life. Guess we move onto the next round."

The Ruthless

Chapter Thirteen

Atticus
Two Years Ago

The restaurant is full of expensive suits and cheap dresses.

The problem with Mounts Bay is that the nightlife is renowned for the availability of drugs and skin. The high rollers come down here for all of the vices they couldn't get away with anywhere else, and there's at least a dozen tables here that hold girls I would wager good money are underage. It's a sickness. A disease in this city that the skin auctions perpetuate.

The seventeen-year-old girl I'm here to meet exits the elevator in a red silk dress that flows down her body like water. I instantly feel like the biggest fucking hypocrite in the world because I would bankrupt myself, drive my business into the ground and set it all on fire, to be the one removing it from her tonight.

It was easier to keep her at a distance when she still looked young and fragile.

She looks like a fucking siren in that thing.

Luckily for me, Ash steps out behind her, ever the watchdog, and stares me down in the most Beaumont way. He could easily pass as a younger Joseph Beaumont Sr. in that charcoal suit, the top button open but with diamond cufflinks no seventeen-year-old should be so at ease wearing.

I curse under my breath.

I can't tell her what I need to with him here. The second the words, 'The Crow' come out of my mouth he'll be throwing her over his shoulder and tearing out of this place as fast as his legs can carry him.

The Wolf will be climbing through my window and slitting my throat before the month is out.

I built my entire residence to be impenetrable thanks to the Jackal's obsession with taking me out, and I'm confident that I've made it as solid as I possibly can… but the Jackal never sent the Wolf after me.

That girl has taken men out that I never thought were possible.

Her connections and her skill sets are unparalleled. If she were a little more confident to stand on her own two feet, she would definitely be the most dangerous member of the Twelve, but the Jackal has broken that confidence in her. Whatever he holds over her head, it's enough to keep her from spreading her own wings and taking this entire city to its knees.

The retribution I'd be facing if I took her out has always made me second guess my choices when it comes to her. I wanted her dead the moment I knew she was heading to Hannaford but then the Butcher had come knocking, letting me know he was still watching out for the kid who risked everything to help him save his wife.

So I watched her.

I watched Avery throw everything she could at her and I watched the Wolf not only survive it, but take that abuse without just killing the girl throwing it at her. The compassion she showed Avery the moment there was an opening for it was more than my beautiful, fierce, broken girl has ever received outside of her close-knit family and I want that for her.

I might not love the idea of there being more killers and criminals in her circle, but even I can admit having the Wolf sleeping in the same room as Avery is a very good thing.

No one will ever get past her.

I stand and pull Avery's chair out for her, ushering for a waiter to arrange another chair and table setting for Ash. Avery smiles at me in a coy way that shouldn't hit me in the chest like a bolt, but it does.

I lean down to kiss her cheek, her hands wrapping around my biceps and drawing me in. She smells fresh and clean and entirely too sweet for all of the things running riot in my head at having her this close to me.

The moment we break away from each other Ash stares

me down like he can tell exactly what I want do to to his sister, everything I've worked so fucking hard to have the chance at having some day.

He'd really kill me if he knew half of it.

"Thank you for coming," I murmur, and Avery smiles at me a little wider as she takes her seat.

The waiter brings over the extra chair right as I hold my hand out for him to take, but he stares down at it like he'd very much like to rip it from my body.

"Ash, please. You promised," Avery says, her voice calm and even which is the most dangerous of all of her tones.

He shakes my hand and then takes his seat, ordering a bourbon immediately and no one questions it. Avery gets a glass of wine the same price as a family vehicle, but there's nothing pretentious in it, her choice is excellent.

As always.

"Is there a reason you wanted to meet or are you still just pretending you aren't panting after her? Fucking pathetic," Ash sneers, flicking his eyes over the menu and just generally bringing down the entire mood of the room. The man at the table next to ours stares at Avery's exposed shoulders for just a moment too long, and when Ash notices, he picks up a steak knife.

"There's nothing that would make me happier than slitting your fucking throat."

The man blanches and wipes his mouth with his napkin, standing up and ushering his date up from the table and out of the restaurant.

Avery smirks back at Ash, "I did need some extra elbow room."

He doesn't smile back, their relationship more strained than I've ever seen it before. "We shouldn't even be down here. There's nothing Crawford couldn't say in a phone call."

I shoot him a look and flick a hand to call the waiter over to take our orders. "I was hoping to speak to Avery privately."

Avery stifles a smile, her eyes darting over to mine. I think I'm softening her anger, getting to her and maybe working my way out of the hole I've dug for myself by keeping her safely away from Mounts Bay.

Ash stares me down, his fingers still wrapped around the knife tightly.

"Over my dead fucking body."

Chapter Fourteen

When we get out of the warehouse, the first signs of the morning sun out on the horizon, Atticus is still directing his men from the parking lot. Luca is nowhere to be seen but the moment Aodhan breaks away from us with a chaste kiss to my cheek, Atticus meets my eye and motions to me to speak with him.

Illi grunts unhappily but leans back on the driver's side door of his car to watch Atticus' every move, a sharp knife in his hand that he twirls idly. He looks relaxed and almost bored as he checks the perimeter, but there's nothing casual about him.

No one would get within ten feet of me without that knife lodging in their throat.

Atticus waits until the Impala is nothing but the roar of an engine in the distance before he speaks to me. "I received another photo today. I need to show it to you and speak with you in private."

I frown. "We can speak here. Illi already knows everything."

Atticus glances over to him and then leans closer into me.

"He knows about the senator? Because Amanda Donnelley does now too."

Fuck.

He hands me an envelope and I barely open it, just peeking inside at the image of Elijah Blakeley, his wife, and two children in there.

Their eyes are all crossed out.

"This isn't good. This is not good at all; Lips is going to come home to deal with this herself," I murmur, and Atticus shrugs.

"Maybe it's time for her to come home. I have Jackson at your ranch right now, fitting the last of the new security in there. It'll be safer than the White House and if you're open to it, I've spoken to an old friend about some improvements to the boundary fencing and gate. It doesn't have to be as extreme as mine but you need something more secure."

I nod slowly. "Can you take me home? We can... discuss this there."

He nods again, glancing up at Illi like he's preparing to fight him but I roll my eyes at him. "I'll speak to Illi; he's not my keeper."

It does take a little convincing before Illi leaves me with Atticus, his eyes full of loathing, but he trusts me to know what the hell I'm doing. I'm not a child and I'm not an object to be guarded and coveted.

If I want to argue with Atticus about our plans to murder

people in the privacy of my own home, I can do it.

I slip into the Bentley and decide I can't stand another second in the Kevlar and strip down to get it off. The windows are tinted dark enough that I'm not worried about any of the Crow's men seeing, and I'm wearing one of my lace bralettes underneath it anyway.

One of the perks of not having a huge cup size.

Atticus slides into his seat right as I pull my blazer back on over the bralette, his eyes burning into my skin as I get it pulled into the right position and buttoned up. I should really put the camisole back on first considering Jackson is back at my house, but so long as the blazer is buttoned up, it's revealing but not obscene.

I'm too goddamn tired for this shit.

"I'd be more comfortable if you kept the vest on until we're inside your house," he says as he starts the car, pulling out smoothly.

I settle back in my seat and message Lips with an update of everything that happened in the Game. All of it vague and entirely in a code that changes so often we're lucky we're both geniuses and can keep up with it. There's nothing any type of law enforcement could take us down for that I couldn't pay our way out of, but there's a lot of other players on the board who would love nothing more than knowing our plans.

"Just because you want it, doesn't mean you'll get it. Hasn't the Bay taught you anything?" I say with a smile, and he doesn't bite back, doesn't flirt with me or argue at all.

He just leans across the car and takes my hand in his. "I'm very good at getting what I want. Almost as good as the ruthless queen everyone keeps whispering about. All I used to hear about on the streets was the Wolf who hid in the shadows and would take you out before you even realized she was there, but now? Now all of the talk is about the girl she trusts with her life and her business, the Beaumont who single-handedly arranged the coup against the Jackal and had her own father slain in his bed while he slept."

I gape at him. "That's not what happened and you know it."

He smirks. "The first rule of infamy is that no one ever gets the details right. That's how legends are started, and that's how a thirteen-year-old girl became the most dangerous person in the city—because she walked out of the Game alive. She was as close to a superhero as you can get to the other kids who have grown up here, and when she chose you to be her friend after being alone for so long? You took on God-like status. That's the real truth of the Bay, Avery. You're a god here until you're not, and now you have the power, everyone is going to try to take it from you. That's the life you'll have now."

I look out of the window at the city passing us by, and his fingers stay tightly wrapped around mine. His words don't change anything. They don't scare me or have me changing a goddamn thing, because my life has always been that way. I've always looked over my shoulder and had to assess every aspect of my life because those around me have been a danger to me.

"I have a family now, Atticus. Everything might be darker and more dangerous now, but at least I'm happy and loved. Ash is happy; fuck, I've never seen him so happy. Harley is alive and happy. Morrison is alive and happy. These are all things that I thought were impossible two years ago. I'm not saying that I'm thrilled at being hunted for the rest of my life, but it's the price I'll pay for our happiness. I'll pay it over and over again."

He doesn't say another word for the rest of the drive but there isn't any anger radiating toward me, no frustration at the situation until we're spilling out into a raging argument.

When he pulls up outside the ranch, Jackson's Porsche is sitting out front.

I really don't want to see him and ruin this moment.

When we unlock the front door, I immediately open up the staircase and usher Atticus down into my panic room. He raises an eyebrow at me but doesn't comment, just steps carefully down the marble staircase, and I hit the lights the moment I can.

His eyebrows hit his hairline at the sight of my murder board.

"It's a work in progress. The missing pieces are over at the safe house, but if everything is cleared for me to come home then I'll bring it back here."

He nods and pulls out the photo of the Blakeley family, waving it in my direction. "Are you going to tell me about him? Another of Grimm Graves' bastard children, and he's on the

Senate."

I shrug. "I'm surprised you didn't notice the resemblance earlier; you've been trying to own him for some time."

He grimaces. "There was something there but I never saw his daughter. She's... well, the girls are definitely where the genes show through."

A dry laugh tumbles out of me as I sit back on the couch, the weight of the entire day falling onto my shoulders. "It was startling in person; there's no way anyone from the Bay could look at Kennedy Blakeley and not know whose blood she is."

"Blood. You're talking like a biker now; the Bay is slowly corrupting you." He pins the new photo up on the wall next to Colt and Chance then stalks back over to join me on the couch. I toe my shoes off and tuck my feet up and underneath myself.

"This is the realest version of myself. This is where I'm most comfortable and happiest. I—Atticus, I never really had a plan for a life that was safe and clean. I don't know how to be that woman. I know you wanted that for me, and I can't thank you enough for everything you've done—"

"I don't want your *thanks*, Avery, I want you alive, safe, and happy. If you insist on being here in the Bay, then I'll have this place wired up to be safer than the fucking Pentagon." He rubs a hand over his face and unbuttons the top three buttons on his shirt.

Those damn tattoos of his are peeking out, and I'm getting desperate to see them finally. I'm about to lean over and just strip the shirt away from him when his phone buzzes again, and he shifts to grab it out of his pocket.

"Jackson is done with the security upgrade. You'll be safe to sleep here again, no need to wait for O'Cronin to come back."

I shouldn't.

I really fucking shouldn't.

But I say it.

"I was hoping you'd stay with me instead."

It feels weird to be leading Atticus up the same set of stairs that Aodhan carried me up, and I have to remind myself that this isn't cheating. Aodhan knows about my feelings, he knows he has to share me, and he gave me back my locket with room in it for Atticus' diamond.

There's still something inherently different about the situation and I can't help but be nervous, worried, *dammit*, scared about it because the one and only time Atticus and I had sex was before my feelings for Aodhan had developed.

It was before I knew that I love him.

I almost want to text him and double check but then I'm opening my bedroom door and leading Atticus in. Everything is perfectly clean. Immaculate really, because even when I've come home to pack bags, I've made sure to leave it looking tidy.

I flick the light on and the moment I attempt to turn around, Atticus is holding my hands by my sides as he slowly steps into my body until he's pressed against me. He's already hard, his hips moving to rub himself against my ass, and I have to bite back a moan.

"Put your hands on the mattress, Avery."

I huff but bend over obediently, planting my hands against the plush white comforter on my bed. He gently nudges my legs wider with his foot, his shoes still on and his hand slowly running down my spine.

"You're not even going to kiss me first?" I say, my voice more breath than substance.

His hands curve down my ass until they find the hem of my skirt, pushing it up and over my hips. "I'll kiss you first, now stop talking. Stop making demands, or I'll make you."

A shiver runs down my spine at the tone of his voice, but I barely focus on the words. There's too much still happening in my brain. I need kissing and foreplay to shut everything out and this abrupt beginning of... well, I'm not even sure what this is the beginning of.

All I know is I want more and I need it to start now.

There's a rustling noise and I glance over my shoulder to see that he's stripping his blazer off, folding it neatly and dropping it onto the plush chaise at the end of the bed. He notices me looking and his hands drift back to my ass, tugging my panties away from one cheek.

Then he slaps me hard enough that I gasp, rocking forward only as far as the grip he has on my panties will allow. His hand strokes over the hot flesh as though soothing the sting away.

"Eyes ahead, mouth shut, legs spread. Do you think you can do that, Floss?"

I shouldn't be enjoying this and I definitely shouldn't be longing for him to keep going, for his hands to keep spanking me until I can't sit right for a week, but I am.

I turn to look back at the wall, shifting a little and widening my stance even more. I'm not sure why exactly I need to spread out so much, but I'm hoping my obedience will earn me what my body is craving.

There's more rustling, more clothes being shed, and I force myself to stay still no matter how badly I want to see those tattoos of his. Or his body, I haven't seen him naked before, and it's been years since I've seen him without a shirt. It makes more sense now, knowing who he is and the tattoos decorating his body, but it doesn't change the fact that his distancing hurt me. Where would we be now if he hadn't pulled away?

I can't think about that either, because that's a rabbit hole of what-ifs and alternate endings that will keep my brain occupied and online for days.

His hands touch me again, tugging at my panties until the crotch rips and then he pushes them further up my waist and out of the way. I'm about to tell him to get the hell on with it when he drops to his knees and spreads me open, his tongue dipping into my pussy as he groans at the taste of me.

Oh God.

Oh *fuck*. I can't help but moan and writhe against his tongue, his hands clamping down over my hips and holding me still until I can't help the words falling out of my mouth. My entire body starts to shake, trembling from the orgasm building up, so close, so close—

He stops and moves away from me.

His hands leave me, his mouth already gone, and I'm ready to cry, or worse.

Beg.

Beaumonts do not beg but maybe just this once I might.

"Atticus—"

"I told you, Floss. I warned you what would happen if you couldn't keep your orders to yourself. I decide what happens in this room between us, not you."

I move to straighten up and tear him a new one because no, that's not how this is going to work, not at all, and his palm cracks down on my ass again, harder this time. My legs almost give out on me, a gasp ripping out of my throat and I feel like I might come just from that.

What the hell is wrong with me?

I seal my mouth shut, biting the inside of my cheek even as he stands up and walks away from me.

Okay, he walks into my closet so it's not like he goes that far away but still, it feels as though he's abandoned me to just stand here, awkwardly bent over, with my pussy fucking weeping for him to come back and finish me off.

It almost kills me, but I do exactly what he's told me to do, not even turning my head when he walks back into the room.

"Shut your eyes, Floss."

Dammit.

I squeeze them shut and his hand caresses my cheek, a reverent gesture. "You can't keep your mouth shut so I've had to improvise. Keep this on and I'll let you come."

They're magic words. I don't even care what he wants me to wear, I'll do it.

Then he slips one of my silk scarves over my head and into my mouth, tying it off at the back of my head tight enough that my mouth can't close around it. I must look obscene, but with my eyes shut I can't see whether he's laughing at me or not, so I just focus on my orgasm.

I kind of want him to spank me again.

Clearly I need therapy.

He waits for a moment, like he's testing me and waiting for me to push the boundaries again. I think I will next time but for right now I need that orgasm; I need that high to wipe everything out of my brain like a giant reset button.

Then his mouth touches me again, diving straight back into my pussy like he's enjoying this as much as I am. When his fingers slip inside of me and his tongue circles my clit, I shatter, my teeth clenching hard on the scarf as I sob. I try to be quiet for him, but there's no holding back the sounds he's coaxed out of me.

When he stands up again, I wait for the sharp sting of his palm against my ass, but it never comes. I wait patiently now that the edge has been taken off, my body more relaxed and pliant. His palm strokes down my ass one last time before he steps back again.

There's more rustling of clothing and the crinkling sound of a condom wrapper, and I wish I could tell him not to bother using one, but I'm too scared he'll stop if I speak and I need him inside of me.

His palm returns to my ass, squeezing and stroking me. "Not a word, Floss. Don't say a word and I'll fuck you until you're screaming around my cock."

I squeeze my eyes shut, locking my body down tight like I'm waiting for it to betray me and ruin this for me, and then I bite back a moan as he pushes in, a tight fit even with my legs spread so wide.

He doesn't ease me into it, his hips just start to move and pound into me until I think I'm going to pass the fuck out. My pussy is still so sensitive, my clit throbbing, and after a few strokes he really does have me screaming out my release.

My hands give way but he shifts his grip and guides my body down onto the bed, facedown with my chest pressed into the mattress by one of his palms. Once the weight of my body is supported by the bed the tremble in my legs turns into a full-blown shake, my entire body dissolving into a quivering mess. His hips don't falter, not even a little, just grinding into me the entire time with the steady control of a fucking long-range sniper.

His hand clamps down on the back of my neck, pushing my face into the bed and I come again with a strangled scream, the scarf doing very little to stifle the sound.

Atticus comes with a groan, his fingers biting into my skin so hard I'm sure I'll have fingerprints in the morning to try to explain to Aodhan.

I lie there, gasping and desperately trying to breathe. He takes a minute to recover and then tugs at the scarf in my mouth, pulling it off and away from me. His hands are gentle as he brushes my hair away from my face, possessive as he slowly removes the rest of my clothes, and reverent as he lifts me up and into his arms.

I've never felt so loved by him before.

Chapter Fifteen

I keep my eyes tightly closed.

"You can open them now, Floss. I can't believe you got through it all without breaking," he says as he walks into the bathroom.

I still don't open my eyes, instead I listen as he runs a bath, fussing with everything while I'm still safely tucked in his arms. I still can't wrap my head around this being Atticus, my Atticus, who I spent so long waiting for and hoping I'd someday make love to.

That didn't feel like making love.

It felt better.

When he climbs into the bath and sits down, settling me into his lap with my head resting on his chest, I finally open my eyes but only because I desperately want to see the markings on his chest that make him the Crow of Mounts Bay.

It's too intricate and gorgeous for a gang tattoo.

The whorls and peaks of the lines hint at feathers without

even really being feathers, and the entire design is in the shape of a crow. I run my fingers down the lines and follow it around, only stopping when I come to a scar on his left side.

The skin is raised and white, definitely an old scar, but it's long and wide enough to have been serious at the time.

Someone stabbed him.

"Stop it, Floss. I can feel you freaking out. I'm alive and it was a long time ago. The man who did it is dead so stop planning retribution."

I glance up, blinking in the bright light after having my eyes closed for so long, and he takes the opportunity to kiss me.

I sigh, my hand cupping his strong jaw because I never want it to end.

I tuck my face back into his chest. "Is it stupid that I feel hurt you never told me? I spent years calling you about every little thing and yet you were off building an empire, an entire life, and being stabbed without me ever guessing. I feel so… small."

He doesn't attempt to defend himself or brush my feelings off. We just lie there together, and I think about all of the paths we could've been on instead of this one.

Then he picks up the soap, lathering his hands up before running them over my body. "I've had to make a lot of hard choices, Floss. Most of them I think I got right. Some I'm sure I got wrong. Then there's the things that I just know I did my best at the time. Keeping Senior busy with the buyers meant that he could play with you without ever involving you. That was all I cared about, just for as long as it took me to build something big enough to take him on and win. It took up too much of my time, but I also trusted Ash, and then Harley when we found him, to keep you safe. He can hate me all he likes, but I knew no matter what, Ash would guard you."

He grabs a washcloth and slowly, sensually, washes me off. It's hard to concentrate completely, especially when his hand dips between my legs, but this moment is too important.

This is the true beginning of the mending from all of the damage his chosen path has done to us.

"The scar is from one of the buyers. Senior enjoyed picking out all sorts of men for me to face and this one was a psychopath just like your brother. He enjoyed knives and he came the closest to getting past me. He tried to gut me, but I killed him before he finished the job."

I swallow around the lump in my throat. "I'm sorry. I'm sorry I've cost you so much."

Atticus presses his lips to my forehead. "This is nothing. It's not even close to what I would pay, give, steal, and slaughter to keep you safe."

I choke out a laugh, sitting up and away from him even as the water sloshes over the edge of the tub. "Why? Why would you do all of that? We were close as children but… how could you know that you'd still want me as an adult? Do you still want me or is this all just a sunk cost at this point?"

He stares at me with a somber expression and his fingertips

run down my spine. "You once broke Bing's foot when we were kids, do you remember that? He flicked Ash's wrist after Joey broke it because he enjoyed hurting people, and when you found out, you stomped on his foot with your riding boots on."

I cringe a little as I remember. My father had beaten Ash until he was choking on blood as my punishment because he knew nothing would hurt me more than Ash's pain and suffering on my behalf. He also hoped it would drive a wedge between us, that Ash would resent me for getting him beaten so badly.

Ash has never, not once, blamed me for our father's many punishments.

I would burn the entire city to the ground for him.

"Then you had photos of Holden choking his high school girlfriend sent to the press, and my father had to pay out her family, because she was an heiress with mafia roots, so they couldn't just kill her to cover it all up. My mother still has nightmares about the entire thing."

I giggle at that because it was some of my best work. I was just barely in middle school but Holden was an absolutely disgusting asshole of a man. Still is.

"There is no being around you, Floss, without desperately wanting to keep you. Without falling in love with your savage, ruthless, perfectly poised self. I've never met anyone who knows their own mind like you do. You make a choice and then you follow it to the very bitter end, no matter the cost. You were mine from the very beginning."

I will not cry.

I absolutely will not cry right now.

He leans forward to catch my chin, drawing my lips into his as he kisses me, slow and deep. It tastes like every word of love and worship he's given me tonight.

His fingers slip back into my pussy again, his other hand curling into my hair gently and holding me still. "Come for me. I want to watch you this time."

His fingers work me over like an expert and his eyes are intense as he takes in my every shudder, gasp, and moan. I thought all of the tension in me had already melted away and that this would be less explosive, but when my eyes drift closed, his fist tightens and he growls at me in the same steely tone, "Eyes on mine. Don't shut them, Floss."

I want to spend the rest of my life listening to these commands.

I come with a groan, trying and failing to stop my eyes from rolling back in my head as I grind down onto his fingers.

Atticus washes me all over again and then lifts me out of the bath as though I weigh nothing, drying me and carrying me back to bed. Once I'm tucked in safely, my eyelids heavy with sleep and every last thought in my brain has been banished by his commands, he stalks back over to his clothes and rummages around in his pockets for his phone.

I drift off to sleep, startling awake again when his fingers thread through my hair and his lips press against mine.

I try to blink away the sleep, but the room is dark and exhaustion is riding me hard.

"Avery, I need to get back to work. Something has come up, but I couldn't leave without saying this. I would do anything for you… but I won't share you. I'm not going to fall into your bed with another man, and I'm definitely not going to work out a sharing schedule of when you can be mine and when you belong to him. I can't and I won't."

And with that, the bubble of happiness and relief and joy bursts.

"Fucking Atticus Crawford, I'm gonna come home and rip his fucking throat out."

I shudder, Lips' words a little too close to home after Lucy's performance in the first round of the Game. "How can I be angry at him though? It's not like polyandry is socially acceptable, let alone a regular thing!"

She huffs down the phone at me. "I'm not talking about that part. I'm talking about where he was totally fine getting his dick wet, but as soon as he got off, he's running the fuck away again? I'll gut him—"

She stops abruptly then curses under her breath.

Then I hear Blaise say, "I'm going to pretend I heard none of that, but you probably shouldn't let me get fucked up around Ash for a bit."

Jesus H. Christ.

"Mounty, tell him I'll reach down his throat and rip his heart out if he says a fucking word to my brother about this."

Lips huffs at me but relays it to him verbatim before walking away, and I hear a door shut and lock. "We're at some shitty fucking hotel in the middle of Texas. I hate it here, everything looks like it's dirty, but there were no other options for the night. Ash is getting fucking blackout drunk with Harley because he's… pissed about Colt."

Ah.

The real reason I needed to call her this morning is because last night Lips met another one of her brothers, the Chaos Demon who's desperate to save the little sister he barely met a decade ago.

I like him.

I'm not surprised Ash doesn't.

Brothers are a trigger for him.

"So? Don't leave me waiting here, Mounty, how did it go?" I say as I lean back on the couch and stare at Colt's photo on the murder wall. After Atticus had left, I'd taken another shower, this one to wake me back up and clear my head. Okay, also to cry in, but that's pathetic and not at all my style.

Then, I made a mountain of coffee and came down here to work.

"He was… fucking terrified of me. He hid it well, but when he realized I was his blood, he freaked the fuck out. I guess rumors of the Wolf's exploits have made it to Texas. He… he was willing to pay anything to keep Poe safe, though, and I offered him whatever he needed. I told him I'd take on Grimm with him if it comes down to that."

I knew I was right about him. "So why is Ash upset about him? Did he say something or is it just his general panic about siblings?"

She groans. "Just general panic. Colt was—he was a loving brother. Rough around the edges, sure, I mean, he's a biker, but he really cares about her."

I nod even though she can't see it. "He met with the Butcher to save her despite their bloody history. That can't have been easy, and you don't do that without really caring about your sister. Ash will get over it. You know he's just overprotective."

She sighs, the squeaking of springs on the hotel bed in the background, and I wince. It must be freaking terrible there. "He'd probably be better about it if I hadn't forced him not to come with me. I met Colt alone, and Harley just watched us with a sniper rifle because he's a worrier."

I laugh at her, a proper roar of laughter that only she can get out of me after the day I've had. "How did you manage that? I literally can't imagine Ash agreeing to leave you alone for anything."

She groans and says, hesitantly, "I threatened to fight them. Ash wasn't prepared to get in the ring with me, and Harley had a little panic about hurting me. Blaise just insisted on me wearing a vest so that was easy enough."

I almost snort with laughter, because of course she did. Of course she found the only kryptonite those boys have and exploited it for her own means. Ash would *never* raise a hand to her, not even to practice or joke around, and Harley spends half his time trying to throw himself in front of her when there's fists being thrown, so that's an instant no.

"I miss you so freaking much, Mounty. How many stops do you guys have left?" I mumble right as my security beeps, and I check on the tablet Jackson left me and see the Impala waiting for the front gates to open.

I hit the button and unlock the front door with a few taps of the screen. It makes things easier and far more secure, but I'm sure Harley will be throwing the tablet at a wall in frustration the second he gets home.

He hates this sort of thing.

"Eight more stops and then I'll be on the way home. I told Ash we should throw money at the driver to just go non-stop until we're home. We could take it in turns. Fuck, I miss my orgy-sized bed and not listening to Finn sleep talk and a real goddamn shower. Oh my God, I miss showers, Aves. The one on the bus is like a fucking cupboard, fuck knows how Harley even fits in there."

I grin while she rambles on as Aodhan's footsteps start down the stairs, a grin on his face as he sees the joy oozing out of me. I hear a door unlock and open down the line, signaling the end of our conversation while Lips has to entertain and babysit one of her many needy men.

"I'll leave you to it. Oh, and Mounty?"

She hums under her breath, distracted at whichever guy has just wandered into her hotel room. I roll my eyes at Aodhan, but it has to be said.

"You would've kicked his ass."

She cackles in evil joy. "Abso-fucking-lutely. I'd own his ass any day of the week."

I hang up, and Aodhan ducks down to kiss me, cupping my cheek gently. "The Coyote did a good job; this place is locked up tighter than a nun's asshole."

I chuckle at him, and he sits down beside me, groaning and leaning back against the cushions like he's carrying the weight of the whole world.

I refuse to think about Atticus right now and how just a few hours ago, we were sitting here and feeling so close for the first time in years. He once again has made his choice, and it's not me. Not really, because my heart is being torn in half right now and if I think about it again, I'll end up on the couch with a pint of ice cream and a movie binge like some pathetic, weak little girl.

Absolutely not.

"Do you wanna talk about it? Whatever the hell has you sighing over there?" Aodhan murmurs, his palm curving around my thigh in a subtle, but clear comfort. He's good at that, the quiet sort of supporting someone without smothering them.

I refuse to live without him.

"Not really. Not right now, anyway. Lips ranted about it enough that I'm angry again and not just fucking moping."

His eyebrows raise. "Cursing? Shit, I'll watch my tone until you're calm again so I don't lose my dick while I'm sleeping."

I scoff at him, but it's more of a laugh than anything. "Your dick is safe. I might go on a killing rampage later, but for the moment, I'm keeping my cool. I have too much work to do to lose my head now."

He nods and stares at the wall for a second before he stands back up and walks over to the MC side of it, lifting his hand and pointing at the Graves boys. "I see it now, you know. They looked familiar, but I just couldn't fucking place it. They're all Lips' brothers. She's Grimm Graves' daughter."

I clear my throat and step over to him. "Yes, but this is top secret. They—there are more siblings. Grimm doesn't know about them, and we have to do everything in our power to protect them and keep them safe. Even knowing this much is dangerous for you, Aodhan. There are a lot of players in this."

He nods slowly. "You're protecting kids, aren't you? I saw your face when you saw the senator's little ones; it was like you were adding them to a protection list."

I blow out a breath and nod. "It is. I can't say anymore than that, but we're working toward… well, we're trying to get Grimm taken out."

Aodhan nods slowly. "So that's why the Wolf is in Texas? To kill him and get his kids clear of his sick games?"

"It's not as easy as that, unfortunately. The Chaos Demons and their spies mean that even if we take Grimm out, there's potentially hundreds of sleeper cells in other MCs ready to take his place and take out the Graves heirs. We're not worried about Colt or Chance, they're grown and can handle themselves, but... the kids."

He curses under his breath and looks back at Blakeley's photo. Kennedy and Carson are both grinning in the posed family photo. There's no way of looking at it without seeing the little girl that Lips should have been. The happy, beautiful, loved little girl.

"I have some contacts I can speak to. They're Demons and dumb as shit, like bragging about shit to people. I've learned a lot in my time about MCs that way so I can see if they know any rats. It's a start, right?"

I lean forward to catch his lips with my own. "Thank you. It's—it means a lot to me."

He presses his forehead to mine and murmurs, "Then it's a priority for us both. Let's fucking fix it."

The Ruthless

Chapter Sixteen

The excellent part of having the security upgraded to DEFCON-1 at my ranch is that I can get ready in my own bathroom with access to my complete wardrobe once again.

The bad part is that it doubles my prep time.

I try on at least eight outfits before I find something that hides the Kevlar without looking bulky or oversized. I slip a gun into my purse but leave the knives at home, confident that I have enough backup for the night.

Illi picks me up and drives us both down to the Game, his fingers tapping on the steering wheel like his skin is crawling.

"Withdrawals?" I murmur, just a little smug.

He shrugs. "That, and there's something wrong about tonight. You don't live in the Bay for as long as I have without being able to smell the bullshit from a mile away."

Great.

I'd thought it was just me struggling with that wired nervous energy. It's as though electricity is crawling through my veins, looking for an outlet and scorching my blood when there's no way for it to get out.

I text Lips.

On our way now, Illi is on high alert as well. I'll call you with updates.

I slip my phone back into my pocket and then sigh, slipping it back out and messaging Ash.

I'm nervous about tonight. I miss you.

His reply is instant. *I can be home in three hours, Floss. Say the word and I'm on my way.*

I've barely finished reading it and he's calling me. "I'm booking a private flight now; where am I meeting you?"

I huff at him even though this is exactly what I need right now. "I'm fine, stay where you are. You guys are due back soon anyway. I just—I just haven't heard your voice in a few days and that makes me nervous. Sorry. How is the tour?"

He grumbles a little, "It would be better if Finn stopped trying to fuck the Mounty and if Lips' brothers stopped showing up out of nowhere."

Jesus H. Christ.

"Ash, I highly doubt Finn is trying anything, because Lips would have said something to me. Jesus, Blaise would have beat the shit out of him and we both know it. You're just pissed off at the close quarters; you're not made for tour buses."

He huffs, but I ignore him and continue, "I met Colt and, as far as bikers go, he's a decent guy. I'm not saying he's never going to be a problem for us, but at least he isn't pure freaking evil. You should trust me a little more."

More huffing. "Of course I trust you, but you're not here to see any of this, and Lips was nervous about meeting him. It might have… affected my feelings a bit."

No shit. "Call me tomorrow? We're almost at the Game, and I need to be my cold self, not Floss. I love you. Don't do anything stupid."

Illi glances over at me as we pull into the parking lot. "He still pissed about the drummer? Harley made me run a background check on the kid. He's harmless."

I roll my eyes. "Stupid, jealous fucking boys. Like I'd let Lips on a bus with Finn without a full screening."

Illi laughs. "There's only room for four in that bed, and they're making sure everyone knows it."

Christ.

When we pull up, we find the Impala waiting for us, and Jack opens my car door, pulling me into a quick hug as he helps me out. It only lasts half a second, but my heart squeezes in my chest.

Everything is going to be fine.

Aodhan tucks me into his side, kissing the top of my head. "Your nominee isn't here yet. We'll wait with you, keep an extra set of eyes out just in case."

Illi nods and leans back against the car, his fingers drumming against his thigh. Jack looks calm and relaxed as he watches the road. The roar of the motorbike can be heard from miles away and at first I assume it's the Boar and his men, but when she turns into the parking lot, it's very clearly Lucy.

Her hair is tucked up into the helmet so when she removes it, it's like every cheesy movie montage ever. The only saving grace is that none of the men here have any interest in her, so I don't have to watch anyone fall at her feet. Illi is happily married, Aodhan only has eyes for me, and Jack is still mourning the death of his pregnant fiancée.

She tucks the helmet into the pack on the bike, stripping the gloves off and shoving them in too before she stalks over to us.

"Sorry I'm late. My cousins tried to run me off of the road like the little pussy bitches they are, and I had to take the long route here. Are you sure I can't take them out before the Game? They deserve it."

Illi huffs out a laugh at her. "We said don't hunt them, not don't kill them. If they're dumb enough to start shit, you can fucking end it."

She rolls her eyes and unzips her jacket until some of her cleavage peeks through. Nothing about her is suggestive or provocative, but there's no denying she's a very attractive woman.

It'll be an asset in the fights, even after last week's bloodbath.

Men never think the bombshell will gut them.

"Let's get in there before the Crow starts some bullshit about us being late," Illi murmurs, and Aodhan kisses my hair again before letting me go, stepping forward and taking the lead with Jack. They're too similar from behind, their strides the same, and Jack makes some joke that Aodhan chuckles about, a dry laugh in the quiet of the night.

"You ready to win, Ammoscato? You better not have any rings on tonight; they'll start a fucking riot," Illi says, falling into step with us both.

Lucy scoffs and holds her hands up, both of them bare. "It's not the element of surprise if they've seen it before."

We step into the warehouse, the same one as last week, and it's already teeming with bodies. After the shock from the losses last week, there's even more punters here to watch the fight and attempt to make some quick cash.

Illi leads us through and we stop, with Aodhan and Jack, only a few feet away from Atticus and Jackson where we'll have a clear view of everything happening.

The crowd parts and moves as the Bear and his nominees make their way past us. I roll my eyes at the sneers and posturing bullshit but then the Bear pauses in front of me, snarling, "You don't belong at the table and soon enough you won't be fucking sitting at it. You won't even be in the fucking city."

I freeze, but he's already scurrying away like the little fucking cockroach he is.

"Did he just fucking threaten you?" Aodhan snaps, and I roll my shoulders back to straighten up.

"Forget about it. He's not distracting us from tonight—" I pause, the words dying in my throat as I watch the Bear hand Atticus a slip of paper and fuck. *Fuck.*

The Viper had chosen the pairings in the last round.

It's the Bear's turn.

"He's going to put them together. He's going to pair two of our three, we both know it," I murmur, and Illi stares him down as he takes his place across the room from us.

"If he does, he's dead. If he does, no diamond is gonna save him from the wrath of the Wolf. Harley will fucking lose it."

I glance over to where Aodhan and Jack are talking but neither of them look worried. I'm actually shocked at how calm Aodhan seems, like this is all following a plan, when really everything is going to shit. I should have just had the Bear killed and asked for forgiveness when the dust settled afterward.

Aodhan notices me looking and tilts his head at me, as close to a reassurance as I'll get from him in this room, filled to the brim with people who would slit our throats and take our place at the round table of the Twelve in a second if they thought they could get away with it.

Illi leans in to whisper to me, "No matter what happens, tonight changes shit. The Bear just threatened you directly, Queenie. He's dead. The Twelve isn't the top threat in the Bay anymore. We are."

I nod and take a half step toward him, letting his body shield me a little more from the smirking asshole across the room. I need the comfort and security of Ash tucking me into his side right now, but Illi is a good stand-in.

I understand why it is that Lips has always been so loyal to him.

"I'm calling the kid when we get out of here. Shit is gonna change around here right the fuck now," Illi snarls, his voice still quiet and meant just for me, but the crowd around us hears the tone and backs away like their asses are on fire. I nod and wait for Atticus to announce the next fight.

He stares the Bear down as well, his eyes a slow and meticulous assessment of just how far this man is going to push us all tonight. Then he looks down at the list and calls out the first names.

In under a minute the fight starts, the first of twelve we have to sit through.

It takes forever, the bigger of the two men intent on actually beating the other man to death, which is not at all a quick process when you're inexperienced.

Ash or Harley could handle it in a third of the time.

One by one, Atticus reads out the list, and every time I don't hear any of our three competitors, my stomach churns more and more.

When ten fights have been held and five dead bodies have been dragged out of the ring, I pray.

I pray that Luca and Lucy have been paired together. I pray that he gives her a swift death and that she feels no pain, because there's no way that Jack will kill a woman. No way, I know it without even looking at him.

"Luca and Jack."

My heart stops in my chest as Illi starts cursing up a storm under his breath. Luca blows out a breath and looks to Atticus. He stares over at the Bear, and I'm about to pull my gun and take the asshole out, end this entire fucking farce right here, but Aodhan slaps Jack on the back as he steps forward and I blanch.

How the fuck is he so calm right now?

They step into the ring and I want to scream. Aodhan's hand slips into mine, squeezing gently as he leans in to me, completely disregarding the audience we have, and murmurs, "He's wanted to die for a long time, Queenie. He wants to go be with Amara, wherever their souls end up, and I can't keep asking him to stay alive for me."

I shake my head, desperate to look away as they both stretch their arms out to show they have no weapons. "He needs a therapist then, not to die! Aodhan—"

He looks down at me and swallows roughly. "He's a man and he makes his own choices. I've spent fucking months wrapping my head around it, but this is where we're at. He told me he'd enter and do what he could. If he won, he'd live. If he dies… he wanted to go out with some kind of fucking bravado so his younger brothers don't hate him for just swallowing his gun. I'm fucking gutted, but what else can I do?"

His voice ends on a ragged note, and I'm about to start *screaming*.

I should have made Ash come home.

He would have stopped this for me. He would've fixed it; he

would have helped me.

Atticus pauses for a little too long before he calls the fight to a start, his hesitation like a wound in my chest because he knows what this is about to do to me and my family.

"Illi, shoot the Bear. Let's just end this now before—"

"Don't do it, Illi. Jack made his choice." Aodhan cuts me off. I want to scream.

I manage to swallow it and choke down the bile creeping up my throat, but no one else around me is freaking the fuck out as we watch Luca very quickly and efficiently *murder Jack*.

Jack does much better than the last guy, landing a fist to Luca's jaw that definitely breaks something with how loud the crack is, but Luca has definitely had the sort of training that Lips has and he takes Jack to the ground, snapping his neck with nothing but his hands.

I'm going to pass the fuck out.

"Fuck, fuck, Queenie, breathe. Breathe. If you don't fucking breathe, I'll call Ash home right the hell now," Illi snaps, and I take a single gasping breath.

Aodhan's hand is clammy in mine, but he's silent, watching as Luca shoves the man who attempts to take Jack's body away and grabs him by the armpits himself.

Atticus waits long enough for them to make it outside of the taped circle before he calls out for the next fight. Lucy doesn't say a word, none of her snarking or bravado, and she drops her jacket to the floor as she steps up. She holds out her arms, but

Atticus barely looks at her before starting the fight.

I watch the entire thing but barely see any of it.

She wins.

I don't know how or why or fucking anything about it, but she wins, and she stalks back over to us to grab her jacket, awkwardly hovering for a second before Illi tells her to get her ass out of here.

I can't look at her or anyone else.

Aodhan's hand is cold in mine.

"C'mon, we're going for a fucking drink. O'Cronin, get moving. We're finding a bar right the fuck now." Illi grabs my elbow and starts to drag me out gently, his eyes savage as he clears us a path without so much as a word.

Every man in here is terrified of what he can do.

It still didn't save Jack.

We get out to the cars and my mind is in a fog. The warm night air does nothing to kick me out of it, not the buzz of my phone in my pocket or the stream of profanity coming out of Illi as he rages about our night.

He doesn't take casualties well.

Aodhan tries to convince Illi that he's going home and doing this alone but the Butcher isn't having any of it, demanding he gets in the BMW right the fuck now so we can find a bar. I don't really know what the fuck to do, so I throw my purse in the backseat and I'm about to slide in when the warehouse roller doors open and people start pouring out. All of the other members of the Twelve start making their way over to the parking lot, and I wince, but then the yelling and screaming starts up.

It's the fucking Bear and his men celebrating their win.

I could throw up.

Atticus and Luca make a beeline for us but I have absolutely zero interest in seeing either of them, and Illi steps directly in their paths.

"Not fucking likely, dickhead. Stay the fuck away before you catch a fucking bullet between the motherfucking eyes."

Atticus glances over at the Bear and Illi's spine snaps up straight, snapping into high alert as the Bear comes fucking charging toward us.

"Slow your fucking roll, cunt, you get any closer and you're fucking dead."

The Bear slows down at Illi's words and starts screaming at Atticus like he can stop the inevitable. "I paid you a diamond; if they kill me, you're fucked, Crow! The Viper and the Ox will know, and you'll have a fucking revolt on your hands."

Pathetic.

The fog finally lifts, burning away with the rage pumping through my veins. I'm untouchable in this moment, if I had my gun there would already be a bullet in his fucking brain.

"The Crow doesn't speak for the Wolf or her family. What you did tonight, the fight and threatening me? Well, you're about to learn all about the real hierarchy in Mounts Bay."

A nervous laughter bursts out of his chest as he looks around desperately, but none of the other members are laughing. No, they're all a little smarter than this idiot and every last one of them has figured it out already.

The Jackal broke the sanctity of the Twelve. He cracked the foundations of the institution and now something else has taken hold in the Bay. A family of people loyal to each other and themselves, fiercely protective of our own agendas. If the Twelve is no longer useful to us then they're out.

The Bear is out.

"You can't do shit—"

I step forward until I'm in his face. "I could slit your fucking throat right here and now and *no one* would do a thing about it. You breathe at my discretion and if you value that oxygen, you'd run. You'd run so far away that the Devil himself couldn't find you because you just made yourself problem number one in my books."

His eyelids peel back until the whites of his eyes are showing but when he looks around, all he can see are the four men caging us both in, ready to pounce and bleed him out the second he attempts a goddamn thing.

"I paid a diamond."

"Your favor to the Crow is nothing to me, and it means nothing to the Butcher. Stag, does it mean anything to you?"

Aodhan answers without hesitation. "Fucking nothing, Queenie."

"There we go. You just keep picking the wrong fucking sides."

I step away from him, mostly because I don't actually have my gun on me and don't have any other options to kill him with, and the moment I turn my back on him, he snarls.

I hear the single gunshot and then a body landing on the gravel.

I turn back to find Atticus staring down at the Bear's corpse, the gun still in his hands.

"So the favors mean nothing now then? The Twelve means fucking nothing," The Ox says, two of his men inching closer to us.

Atticus shakes his head and snaps, "No, it means that I'm not going to put up with a second Jackal. Stick to your own fucking business, stay out of each other's shit, and we'll be fine. Don't mess with the fucking Family."

"Of course you'd fucking say that! Looking after your own fucking people," the Viper snarls and stalks off toward his car, his own men following quickly after him like they're glad to be clear of this shitshow.

Atticus doesn't glance our way at all, just stares down all of the other members until they walk away. "I'm not a member of the Family. I'm just smart enough to see the writing on the wall."

Chapter Seventeen

Illi gets Aodhan so wasted he has to help me carry him back up to the loft.

When I tell him no one is supposed to know about it, Illi shrugs. "There should always be a fail-safe and now Jack's gone, that's me. I'm gonna—Queenie, Luca didn't put him in the acid. I'm gonna go pick him up, and we can get him on ice until the O'Cronins decide what the fuck to do with him. I'm sorry, kid. We shoulda just killed the fucking Bear and dealt with the consequences."

My eyes fill with tears again. "You heard Aodhan… he made his own choices."

Illi huffs and pours Aodhan onto the mattress for me as I hit the light. He's already snoring lightly, something he never does, so I start panicking about him choking on his fucking tongue.

"We both know his decision was a shit one. A really fucking shit one because now you're crying and Aodhan's gonna go fucking feral. You don't lose people without losing your head."

I nod, but we all made our choices tonight. The wrong ones. I should've just said something. I should've been the one to put an end to it, goddammit!

"You need me to hang around? Is there a couch I can pass out on, keep you company?" Illi looks around, but it's still pretty bare.

"I'm fine, Illi. Thank you. Thank you for taking us out and for—for getting Jack. You're a good man."

He gives me a grin that's more of a grimace, raking a hand through his hair. "Not really, kid. I'd just do anything for family and… this shit is hard. Lock up after me, I'll keep some eyes in the area just in case there's retaliation."

Jesus.

I nod and do as he says then I strip Aodhan down to his boxers. It's difficult with him as a dead weight but when it's done, I grab a bucket and then tuck the comforter around him.

I head into the shower to clean away what I can of this night. I don't want to, but I stand there under the stream of water and sob. I sob because Aodhan has so few people left who he trusts, so little family, and he had to let Jack go. I cry because Jack guarded me with such respectful care, coming to my aid without question because I was his cousin's girl.

I cry because he hugged me before we went in, like he knew it was the last chance he had to.

And then when I step out of the shower, pressing the towel to my face and breathing in the clean scent, I cry because I have to call Harley and tell him.

Even though I have pajamas here, I pull one of Aodhan's shirts and a pair of his sweatpants on. I grab my phone and then I crawl into the bed, trying not to rock him too much.

I don't want him to wake up and see the mess I'm in. I don't want him to put aside his grief because I'm splitting fucking open and spilling out everywhere.

I'm going to be strong for him tomorrow.

Illi called. I'm coming home.

I glance over at Aodhan but he's still snoring, so I take a chance and hit dial on Harley's number.

"I'm coming home, Floss."

"I'm sorry. I'm so sorry, I should have just had him taken care of earlier. Harley—"

"Stop it. I know you, Floss, I know you did everything you could—"

"I didn't though! I could have stopped it, I could have—"

"What? What could you have done in a warehouse packed full of Mounties and Twelve members? You had Illi and Aodhan as backup, that's it, Aves, what could you have done about it?"

The words stick in my throat, the fight in me fizzling out until all that is left is the sobbing. Harley, the man who just lost his cousin, stays on the line with me for over an hour while he coaxes me out of my breakdown. He quietly and patiently talks me down until I can breathe again.

I fall asleep to the sound of his voice.

Aodhan sleeps until the afternoon, finally getting up and taking a shower when I agree to cook him a greasy breakfast to soak up his hangover.

Illi and Lips both spend the day messaging me, checking in on us both. I convince Lips to stay away, but only because I don't want anyone bothering Aodhan until he's ready to face the world again.

He looks like shit when he sits down at the breakfast bar to eat.

I make us both coffees but he doesn't touch his, just eats and then climbs back into bed. I hand him some aspirin and then I leave him the hell alone so he can wallow and process by himself.

I stare at the wall instead.

The photos I'd brought over are still pinned up there, and I make myself a second coffee to sit and stare at them for a minute.

There are too many unknowns up there. There are too many things where we're waiting on someone else to show their hand, and I'm ready to do what I know needs to be done, not what's right.

Fuck what's right.

I want Amanda Donnelley dead. And Grimm Graves, the entire fucking perverted Crawford family. I want to wipe the board clean and start over. I want to flush out the turncoat

Twelve members to make sure they never come after us again.

I *never* want to see Luca again.

I take notes on my phone, saved in a highly encrypted file, of all of the leads that I'll be looking into. I don't just stick to the main issues, I delve into every little part of each person's life and pick through everything that could help me.

By the third cup of coffee, Aodhan finally resurfaces again, his face blank but his eyes are bleary. He looks tired but that bone-weary type of exhausted that doesn't come from lack of sleep.

It comes from losing your best friend.

"Do you want some coffee? Pancakes? A steak?"

He huffs and stretches until his back cracks and pops. "Do we even have a steak in the fridge? I'm fine, Queenie. I need a shower and a shave, then I might be human again."

He stumbles off to the bathroom, shutting the door quietly behind him. Everything about him is muted, deflated, and just quiet. I get it and I'm not expecting anything at all from him, but it's still fucking heartbreaking. I would do anything, anything, to go back in time and take the Bear out before he could write that fucking list of his.

I hope he got thrown in a tub of acid.

I need to ask about that.

There's not much else I can do with the pictures and boxes of information I have here, so I pull myself up off of the floor and wash my coffee cup. Then I wipe down every last surface area in the kitchen, sweep, mop, and wipe over the glass on the oven door.

When the shower finally shuts off, I peel the rubber gloves off of my hands and take a seat on the mattress to wait for him. I feel… lost. Like I'm waiting around with nothing to do, but with a mind that won't stop spinning until I think I'm going to pass the hell out. I can't leave here and get back to work, or tear my house apart to quiet the storm brewing in my head, but I also can't stay here and slowly but surely go insane.

Is this what grief feels like? I've never had to grieve someone like this. The only person I really cared about who died was my mother and I was a child… and also terrified because I knew my father had done it and he immediately began his psychological warfare on Ash and I.

I didn't have the time or the maturity to grieve.

The bathroom door opens and interrupts the spiraling panic building in my brain. Aodhan is cleanly shaven and fully dressed, but he still looks absolutely wrecked.

I smile sadly at him and he drops down onto the mattress next to me, his fingers threading through mine. "I've gotta go see the family. Cian and Patrick need to be told in person and we need to decide where we're burying him."

I nod and run my fingers through his hair, pushing it back and out of his eyes. It's all messy and unruly from the shower, and he hasn't bothered taming it.

I don't blame him.

"I'm going to head home for a few hours. There's some files there I need and I need to… clean. I need to organize for a few hours."

He nods, his eyes drifting over to the window-slash-door. "I'll drive you home, see you in safe. I'll come stay with you tonight if I can. I don't know how this is going to go down; I might take a leaf out of Illi's book and just get them both fucking wasted."

I smile ruefully because, well, we both survived the night thanks to that tactic. I was able to focus on Aodhan and he could focus on *not* focusing, so clearly, there's a method to that madness.

"How old are his brothers? How old was Jack?" My voice breaks saying his name, but I say it anyway.

I'm not going to let him fade away.

"Twenty-one. He was six months younger than me. Cian is eighteen and Patrick is seventeen. They've both been working for the family, doing what they can to get us back on our feet. Cian is seeing a girl from the slums; he's been trying to get her off of the streets and staying with us, but she's worried about the O'Cronin reputation. Makes sense, she's too street smart to just listen to some guy she's messing around with. Patrick is… wild. He's been dying to come to parties at the docks but Jack put his foot down about it. I think he was worried about him getting his drink spiked and stolen out from under us."

I giggle because it's all painfully sweet. "So Patrick is too charming for his own good? Noted."

He smirks and blows out a breath. "He's the spitting image

of Uncle Éibhear. Too pretty to be left alone for long and he knows it, too. I keep waiting for the day some angry pops will show up with a shotgun because he's been bed-hopping."

I cackle, because he sounds like some old man talking about his grandkids, but I guess that's what it's like being the head of your family.

"What was Amara like? What was Jack like when they were together?" I whisper, and he slumps down on the bed. I stretch out next to him like a cat, cuddling up close to listen to him, to honor his blood with their stories.

That's how they live on.

"Amara was… she was terrified of our family. She lived two streets over from us when we were kids, and Jack was fucking besotted by her. Fuck, he'd follow her around school and the streets like a lost little puppy. She hated him. Fucking hated him… until she didn't and then he lost his shit because we all knew it wasn't safe to bring a girl home. Not unless she was Irish and from a family that our fathers did business with. So we kept her a secret. A year at high school together before he dropped out to work full-time, he never once let it slip to anyone about her."

I hum under my breath. "Harley knew about her though. I didn't know you guys were close enough to tell him that."

He groaned and rubbed a hand over his face. "Harley covered for him. He saw him sneaking home one night and when Colm started fucking screaming at him, Harley went and covered for him. I'm sure he just did it because he hated us all and wanted any excuse to punch one of the uncles, but Jack thanked him and told him. Not her name or any details at first but… eventually he did."

He presses his nose into my hair, breathes me in like it'll help him get through the day. "Amara's parents were broke. Too many kids to feed, and the second she finished high school, they kicked her out. I helped Jack get an apartment for her and he worked night and day to save for them both. She was going to beauty school during the day and doing all sorts of jobs whenever she could to keep them going. She was the best fucking thing to happen to him, and they took her from him… just to keep him from being happy."

I swallow, clearing my throat. "They deserved worse than they got. They deserved so much worse."

He nods and then chuckles, wiping a hand over his face. "Lips asked where we buried them. Said she wanted to dig them up to piss on them. Fuck, I've never been so shocked and impressed than I was by that fucking meeting. Harley and her were just joking around but that's when I knew that she was perfect for him too. He never smiled and laughed like that back home."

I fake gag. "She totally wouldn't. She'd ask Blaise to do it for her, he'd get a kick out of it. She used to hate it when Harley would pee in the bathroom while she was showering back at Hannaford."

He groans. "What kind of a fucking school is that? Harley was off having orgies and Michelin star meals while I was learning geography bullshit from a ninety-five year old veteran whose benefits were cut off. What an asshole."

I sit up again and then lean down to kiss him, just a peck because the sun is setting and he needs to go break the news to his family. His eyes stay closed for a second, like he's holding onto this quiet moment desperately because the moment it's over, the real world will filter in and he'll have to face that Jack is gone. Then he opens his eyes and smiles at me, but it doesn't reach his eyes.

"Time to go home, Queenie."

The Impala is quiet the entire drive, my phone on silent in my pocket and Aodhan's hand on my thigh like I'm a comfort to him. He leaves the radio off and just stares out into the night.

"Let me know if you go anywhere tonight. Message me or something, I'll still try to come home to you otherwise," he murmurs as we pull up to my gate. I hand him the security sensor to get him through and then the moment we park, he gets out to walk me inside. It's sweet, and he's always done it, but I get the feeling he's trying not to be overprotective right now.

I couldn't handle it. Not from him and not even right now while we're all on high alert.

"I just want to have an early night, I think. I'll be up working in the morning, maybe just stay home for the night and focus on getting everyone through tonight. I'm a big girl, Aodhan. I'm not going to be a burden to you."

He side-eyes me and then tugs me into his arms, kissing me slow and deep just long enough that I know he means business. "You're never a fucking burden, don't start that shit with me, not while I don't have time to prove to you just how wrong you are. Go to bed, get your rest and I'll be back in the morning for whatever the hell you feel like cooking me. You're everything to me, Queenie. You're the light in my darkness right now."

I swallow and take a second to be brave. "I love you, Aodhan. Please come home safe to me."

His eyes squeeze shut and he leans down to press his forehead to mine. "I love you too, Avery Beaumont. Stay here and stay safe for me too because if I lose you, I'm going the same way as Jack, I swear to fucking God."

I nod and give him one last kiss before he leaves, my heart walking out the door with him.

Chapter Eighteen

Another photo was posted on my door this morning. Can you meet with me, we need to talk about this.

I stare down at the text from Atticus as I brush my teeth. There's no way I can deal with seeing Luca right now, and I'm not sure Atticus will go anywhere without him after he's just killed another member of the Twelve. I imagine his security has tripled at the very least, and he'll have a lot to say about me driving anywhere alone.

Haven? Come alone.

A drive out to Haven will clear my head. I could take one of Ash's Ferraris and make a real adventure out of it, let off some steam. I snort at myself for even thinking it, because if anything was going to push him over the edge to come home to me, touching his cars would be it.

I'll take the Rolls Royce.

I'll see you there.

I take my time in getting ready. Whatever this information is that he has for me, I'll deal with it and then I'm going to discuss dating him. I've spent a lot of time thinking it through, even when I was desperately trying not to, but something about losing Jack has made things a little clearer to me.

I can't live without Atticus, but Aodhan has become non-negotiable to me.

He's going to have to live with that. If anyone can convince two men who loathe the sight of each other to share a woman, it's me. There doesn't have to be schedules or negotiations, no actual threesomes or physically sharing. I can live between the two of them until we can reach an agreement.

If three egos the size of Ash, Harley, and Blaise's can figure it out, we can too.

I call Lips. "I'm meeting with Atticus about some new information."

She groans. "Are you or is this a booty call? We have six shows left, Aves, and then Ash is going to be crawling all over your shit again. I was kind of hoping you'd be settled when we got back and we could just… tell him to get over it."

There's a huff and then a grunt. Blaise is with her and she's elbowed him for interrupting us. I roll my eyes, but if she trusts him to keep his mouth shut then I will to.

"I'm going to tell him he has to accept how this is going. I'm sick of hearing his opinions on things; this is what we're going to do."

Lips cackles and Blaise mutters, "How do you think that's

going to go? Let's put money on it."

I'm going to snap at him, threaten his life and dick a little, but Lips snarks back, "She's Avery fucking Beaumont. If she wants it, she'll get it."

"Marry me, Mounty. Let's just run away from these assholes and go be happy somewhere together. I'm thinking tropical, lots of cocktails, and a pool to float in."

She laughs at me, and there's a scuffle down the line as Blaise retaliates in a way that I'm sure is sexual.

Pervert.

"If the two of you are about to fuck then I'm leaving. I've heard enough of that in the last two years for an entire lifetime, thank you very much."

Lips groans like I'm killing her and Blaise roars with laughter, probably at the blush on her cheeks, because she might be the most dangerous person in all of Mounts Bay, but she still squirms in embarrassment over the smallest things.

It's endearing and ridiculous.

"So you're meeting with Crawford and then coming home? Or his place? How long should I leave it before I send Illi in to rescue you from the Crow's dungeon?"

She says it with a teasing tone, but we both know it isn't a joke. I swipe my lipstick over my lips, a red slash of color because men are all the same and spend half their time thinking about that color smearing over their dicks. "Forty-eight hours. Give me two days and then send Illi in. Aodhan... Aodhan went home to the O'Cronins to tell them about Jack and make some arrangements."

Lips hums softly. "Harley told me. Aodhan is going to wait until we're back to bury him since we're only a couple of weeks away. He argued with Harley to keep him here."

I smile softly. "He's buying me more time to sort Atticus out. He's too considerate sometimes."

She scoffs at me. "He'd fucking want to be because Atticus is the most arrogant, inconsiderate asshole I know and you need some fucking balance."

I roll my eyes. "If you come home just to climb in his window and slit his throat, I'll never forgive you."

"Lies. I could shoot his entire house up and you'd only slap my wrist. Listen, you're a big girl and you can handle your own shit. That's why Harley backed down, he knows you're your own person."

I smooth a hand down my dress and turn slightly in the mirror to assess everything one last time. "Ash might not recognize the sister he comes home to… I've done a lot of growing since you guys have been gone."

"People tend to do that when they finally get to stand on their own two feet."

When I hang up with her, I call Aodhan, but he doesn't pick up so I send him a quick text to say where I'm going, that I love him and I'll see him in a few days.

He messages back without hesitation.

The bar is so loud I missed your call, sorry Queenie. Be safe and call me or Illi for anything. I love you too.

I slip on a pair of heels, grab my purse, and head out to the garage. I triple check the security feeds and make sure everything is all in order before I get into the Rolls Royce and then I check the glovebox for the spare gun Lips stashed in there for me.

Two guns, a Rolls, and red lipstick. This feels like a date.

I giggle at myself and then head off, putting the new Vanth album on and singing along at the top of my lungs because there's no one here to see how freaking ridiculous I look. There's a reason they're currently touring the country with sold out shows for every stop because Blaise's lyrics are incredible and his voice pulls at your chest until every last emotion he's coaxing out of you just pours out. I'm not quite as obsessed as Lips and Ash are but I still know every word to every song.

When the duet with Lips comes on, I have to choke back tears the whole time because I'm so proud of her and her voice is hauntingly beautiful.

I make the drive in good time, the roads a little less congested than they usually are at this time of night. The strings of lights in the trees that line the streets make the entire little town look like something out of a storybook fairy tale. I remember the first time I came here I thought there had to be something dark or sinister behind the little town, like a serial killer or two, but for our entire schooling lives it was just a quaint little place to come to during weekends. Once we hit high school, it became the place where the guys would sneak off to and drink at the bar.

The chili cheese fries are a disgustingly delicious mess that even I can appreciate after a margarita or two.

I'm far too tempted to go get some and send a picture to Harley to gloat.

The small park is in the center of the town and every inch of the playground and lawn can be seen from the parking lot. I immediately know something is wrong and dread pools in my veins, the relaxing and joyful drive ruined in an instant.

His car isn't here.

I immediately hit the locks on my car doors, even as I put the car in park and let it idle. I've never, ever come to meet Atticus and beat him to the location. He isn't just on time to meetings, he's chronically early to the point that I always assume he arrives a full hour before and just… enjoys the quiet. A commodity that as the Crow, he doesn't get much of.

He should be here.

Jesus H. Christ, what if someone has kidnapped him? Panic starts up in my gut. I reach for my phone right as a shadow comes over my side window. They move too fast for me to look over, thank God, because suddenly the glass is blown out and raining down on me.

A squeal rips out of my throat and I reach for my purse, but they've caught me unaware and completely unprepared, a stinking rag pressed over my mouth and nose before my brain has even registered what the hell is going on right now.

I'm being fucking kidnapped.

And then I'm out.

I come to in the trunk of a car, trussed up like a freaking Christmas turkey, and my stomach is roiling with the aftereffects of whatever the fuck they knocked me out with.

Who the hell chloroforms people these days?

I thought that was just an old relic of bad thriller movies, not a real way of freaking kidnapping someone. I had no idea that the fumes would make me feel so sick, and the motion of the car only makes things ten times worse.

The gag in my mouth isn't the worst thing, though I don't want to think about Atticus right now and if he's lying dead in a ditch somewhere because nothing else can explain why he didn't meet me. The worst thing is the bag over my head.

I've spent a lot of time over the last few months working on the trauma of what the Jackal forced me to do and exactly zero time working through what it felt like to be kidnapped by Diarmuid. He'd arrived at my bedroom door back in senior year with a flirty smirk and a bag tucked in his back pocket. We had no freaking clue that he'd bargained with the Jackal to hand me over, that he had betrayed us all, so I'd just opened the door to him and listened to the lies he'd drawled out.

The moment I turned my back the bag was over my head and my wrists and ankle were cable tied.

I screamed out but he was much bigger than me and just slapped a hand over my mouth, pressing the filthy fabric into my mouth until I was too busy trying not to vomit to scream.

The car trip was a nightmare.

He'd spent the whole time trying to convince me that this was all my own fault. That Harley was an O'Cronin and I'd softened him. He might not have been complicit in the abuse that happened in the compound but he definitely agreed with half of their crackpot fucking sexist views.

Harley couldn't possibly be a real man if he valued women.

He couldn't be strong and capable if he went along with plans that Lips and I had made, because women don't belong in conflicts. He had talked about Lips like she was a parlor trick, like she was nothing more than a talented magician who didn't really hold any power.

I still hate thinking about him.

The differences in my kidnapping this time are that only my hands have been tied and I've been placed in the trunk of the car. I part my legs a little and tense them when the car takes corners so I don't roll around too much. I can hold the position forever if I need to, my legs are the strongest part of my body, and that helps a little with the panic clawing up my throat.

I do a lot of deep breathing and planning.

This has to be either Amanda Donnelley or one of the members of the Twelve—the Viper or maybe the Ox. It could possibly be one of the Crawfords, pissed at Atticus and retaliating by taking me.

Then the car comes to a complete stop and I snap my legs back together.

I'm so goddamn pissed at myself for wearing a skirt. I might burn them all the second I get home, because they're an easy-access item of clothing and I'm desperately trying not to think about what is going to happen to me here.

Those same rough hands pull me out of the trunk, tugging at the bag to adjust it and ensure it's still in place and blocking out all light. It also muffles sound fairly well but there's an echo, so we're obviously walking through a parking garage. It's difficult to concentrate on the little details with how raw my entire brain feels thanks to my chloroform nap, but I push myself to start cataloging everything.

This is how I'm going to get out of here.

I don't need a white knight, I need to pay attention because Aodhan isn't going to come storming in after me this time. He won't even know I'm gone, I'd told him not to expect me home and to stay at the compound for *a few days*.

Will I still be alive in a few days? Aodhan's words ring in my mind, as clear to me now as when he spoke them to me just hours ago.

If I lose you, I'm going the same way as Jack, I swear to fucking God.

Absolutely not, I'm going to survive this and go home to him. I will not be the victim this time around; I'm so fucking sick of being the target and the easy pickings for these people.

We pause for a minute, the hand around my arm tightening and then an elevator bell rings. Hotel or an apartment complex, my guess is the latter. The man, definitely a man from the feel of his walking and the size of his hand, tugs me into the elevator. I wiggle my hands again but the bindings barely have any give in them. My hands feel a little numb, like the circulation to them has been cut for too long and then I have to push down another wave of panic.

What if I have permanent damage?

Stop it, Beaumont, focus.

The elevator bell chimes again and out we step, my feet dragging but not doing much to slow us down with his rough treatment of me. There's not much else to go on. We only walk for another seven seconds before he stops and pulls out keys, the jingling sound of them unmistakable. Then a door unlocks and we're walking again.

The room we walk into is too warm. There's either no thermostat or this man is cold-blooded, because even in the skirt, I'm starting to sweat almost instantly. He drags me along and then stops, jerking me around and shoving me back until I stumble away from him awkwardly.

He does something to the ties around my wrists and they loosen, not falling away but I feel a glimmer of hope.

Then there's a weird sliding noise around me, a loud click, and then nothing.

Nothing.

You forget how much sound is really in a quiet room until it all just disappears, and the only sound I can hear now is the thumping of my own heart as it beats an erratic tune in my chest. It's as if I stepped into a freaking vacuum. The sweating gets worse and I tug at my restraints, surprised when they fall away from me.

I scrabble at the bag, tugging it off and ripping at the gag.

My eyes start streaming at the bright light and I blink rapidly, my arms coming in front of my body like I'll have any chance to defend myself right now.

Glass.

I'm surrounded by glass.

There's a buzzing sound and then a voice comes through a speaker, though I can't see where it is. "You really do look like a little birdie in there."

I rub at my eyes again, cursing under my breath as I try to find the man, but there's nothing but an empty apartment in front of me.

Little birdie.

Jesus H. Christ.

"Interesting woman, Amanda Donnelley. She can find anything a man would ever want. She was friends with my father; they both enjoyed curating collections."

Fuck.

Fuck, that's where the photos came from. I stare back out at the bare walls and carpets, but he's nowhere to be seen.

"When she hired me to follow you... well, I recognized you. My father once tried to add you to his collection. Such an exquisite example of Russian-American bloodlines. Did you know that? If you trace the Beaumonts back far enough you hit royalty. That can be problematic, what with the many diseases and defects, but you've been bred beautifully. Those cheekbones! I heard you have a twin, such a shame it's a male. Males do not display well. There's always issues with them."

I look around, but there's piles of crap around me that don't look helpful right now. A pile of blankets, a desk, some books... no speaker and the glass distorts the sound so I can't figure out where it's coming from.

The glass surrounds me on all sides.

"To think I almost lost you to the Crow. Atticus Crawford, the man who murdered my father. Paid a diamond to the Wolf to get rid of him. He couldn't find my father's place, you know? He couldn't find it then and he won't find my apartment either. I've been too careful. By the time the Wolf comes home, it'll be too late for you. Everything happens for a reason, Avery Beaumont. You slipped away from my father then because you were always meant for me. The first of my own collection."

The Ruthless

Chapter Nineteen

The glass is all one sheet without any joins or weak spots. It's thick enough that pounding on it with my fists makes no sound, an eerie thing to see in action. I can't see how the hell it opens and closes, only the noises I'd heard as he put me in here as clues. There's no hatch for food and only a bucket in the corner that I'm assuming I'm supposed to pee in, but I'd rather die.

I would rather die.

I stand there and wait for the man to come back and do something but time crawls past me with nothing. The space I'm in is filled with items, and there's a small wooden chair and desk pushed up to one side. I pull the chair out to look around the room beyond the glass.

This isn't the only glass enclosure but none of the others have prisoners or items in them. One of them on the far side is open, but it's too far away to make out any clues on how to get them open.

I'd never thought to ask Lips how she'd done it.

I start to look through all of the items, just in case there's something that might be a help to me. There's no bed, only a pile of blankets and pillows in one corner that smell musty and old. I would be forced to peel my own skin from my body if I touched any of them, so beyond poking at them with the toe of my shoe, I forget about them entirely.

There is a collection of books. None of them are hiding a weapon or key in them, and they all look as though they were borrowed from a library in the '80s and never returned. There's a candle, a bowl, some little china figurines, and a bottle of water.

I'd kill for some water, but I'm not ingesting a goddamn thing in here.

The bucket is haunting me from the corner.

The more I look, the less I find and when I'm flipping through the books for the third time, the panic finally consumes me. My breathing speeds up until I'm gasping for air and still getting none. My heart feels as though it's about to burst in my chest and my vision starts to white out around the edges.

It's a full-blown anxiety attack.

I can't pass out here, what if the man is watching me? What if he comes back in here after I'm out and touches me? There are too many bad options here.

Months ago while I was feeling particularly terrible about myself and how I'd handled everything that had happened in the Jackal's lair, I'd asked Lips about it.

About the secret to surviving everything.

"How do you get through it? How do you work through something that painful? When the Jackal cut up my feet I—Lips, I thought I was going to pass out dead on the ground."

She had smiled at me sadly, looking uncomfortable to be talking about her trauma but always open and honest with me when I needed it. "You have to find something you can really focus on. It has to be something that isn't an easy thing or something that doesn't mean shit. It's like… so Illi once told me he goes through the correct way to butcher a pig. The whole process from slaughter to plate. I count down from a hundred in French, because numbers were always the hardest part of the language for me. It has to be something you know but that is complicated enough that it can keep your brain busy."

It sounded simple enough, but it had taken weeks before I found the thing that my brain could hold onto, even when everything else is blocked out, to work through until the pain or panic subsides.

I work on recipes.

Not just the general ingredients lists of boring things like oatmeal cookies. No, I work my way through my entire cookbook. Years ago, Ash had bought me a huge leather-bound blank journal that he had joked about, calling it my *magnum opus*. Blaise called it my spell book, and in the dining halls at Hannaford, Harley used to joke loudly that it was bound in human skin; a sacrifice of worthless, gossiping little sluts who got in my way.

Every recipe I love goes in the book with photos and reviews. If something goes wrong I make a note. If someone else in the family has a popular request, it goes in the book.

I know it back-to-front.

So I sit there on the tiny and uncomfortable wooden chair and start to work through the book, reciting not just the names of the dishes and the basics of how to make them but also the variations and notes. I recite the changes I've had to make because of the differences in the oven operation from Hannaford to the ranch. I picture the plates that I use for each dish, because I would never serve a carved roast beef on the same serving dish as a broccoli gratin, or a stack of blueberry pancakes on the same shaped plate as French toast with ice cream and sprinkles.

I watch through unfocused eyes as the sun sets, working my way slowly through the entire recipe book and when I finally come to the end, my heart is beating normally. My chest still has a dull ache but I can breathe around it. The anxiety is still there and I doubt it will leave me until I get the hell out of here, but I can now think around it. I can acknowledge it's there without being consumed by it.

Now that it's dealt with… how the fuck am I getting out of here?

With no clock in the room, I have no fucking clue how long I sit there and just stare into nothingness. I'm used to sitting for long periods of time and working, but without my phone there's limits to what I can keep busy with.

I miss my phone.

I miss all of the information in there that would keep me busy for months. I'd just gotten a new file full of the arrest and warrant records of the Unseen down in Coldstone. King Callaghan absolutely without a doubt in my mind went down for a crime he didn't commit and there is a long, stinking trail of dirty cops and judges who have kept him in that prison for this long.

What I wouldn't give to be looking for patterns in the paperwork right now.

Because the glass cell is soundproof I don't hear the door on the far side of the apartment open, so the movement startles me. The man who walks in is entirely average and forgettable. The type of man you could see in a crowd a hundred times and still never notice anything about him.

His glasses are clean but a little too low on his nose, and while he has broad shoulders and toned arms, he also has a little bit of a beer gut hanging over his pants, the type that says guilty midnight snacks are obviously a staple in his pantry. Hair the color of dirt, eyes a little too small for his head... he's just some middle-aged guy.

I loathe the sight of him.

He lifts a walkie-talkie up to his lips and says, "You look so pretty in there, little birdie. You were made to be collected."

His eyes drag over my body and I cross my arms over my chest, covering what I can from his eyes. I'm still wearing the blazer and camisole, even with the heating making me feel like I might die. He's obviously turned it up to get me to strip down, but I refuse.

He walks up to the glass, pressing his entire body against the length of it and peering in at me. I want to slam my fist against the glass, but it'll only break my hand and I need to be smart right now.

He lifts the walkie-talkie to his mouth again, his lips too close so the sound is a little distorted.

"My father never spoke to his collection. He just locked them away and watched them slowly break down. Did the Wolf ever speak of them? Did she know all about the careful curation she ruined? My father had spent decades finding the right bloodlines. *Decades*. Do you have any idea how hard it is to find pure bloodlines *and* a perfect package?"

I really couldn't care less about his drivel, none of it helping me to escape and none of it even the slightest bit interesting. Why is it always the self-important, arrogant, perverted men that ramble on for hours? I don't care what Illi said about it, from the way he's pressing himself against the glass I can tell that it's only a matter of time before he's going to jerk himself off out there or do something else fucking disgusting.

I fucking despise men.

He rambles on and on about the beauty in me, the perfection

and how freaking delicate I am. He's just the next man in a long line to take a look at me and stick me in a box. Spoiled, pampered, rich brat who doesn't like to get dirty. They all think I'm weak.

Every last one of them.

I bite my tongue so hard my mouth fills with blood, and I can't stand listening to another second of his bullshit tirade so I finally stand up, rolling my shoulders back and stepping up to the glass. His words don't falter as he watches me, describing how much of a lady I am.

I spit my blood out onto the glass.

You'd think I shot at him the way he recoils, horror etched into his face and finally his words come to a screeching halt. He takes a step back and then another. The claustrophobic feeling eases off a little in my chest.

I watch the blood slowly slide down the glass, and it's a disgusting but necessary evil right now.

I couldn't stand to hear his voice for a second longer.

"That's not—you're not supposed to do that. This is your home now; you can't mess it up."

I don't want to listen to anything else this freaking psychopath has to say, but there's no getting out of this glass enclosure without some clues. If he's planning on keeping me alive, he has to feed me somehow, and I need to have a plan for when that happens.

He starts a whole new tirade about what's expected of me in

here. The sound bounces around the glass hell he has me locked in, and I feel that familiar *snap* inside my brain.

There goes the sane and rational girl.

I need to destroy everything. Start fresh after the destruction, after everything has been wiped away to make room for the calm again. I need to tear everything to the ground before I lose my fucking mind.

When I pick the bowl up and smash it against the ground, the man startles again, even though he probably can't hear the sound of the crash, and then he turns on his heel and flees as though he's running scared.

Fucking pathetic.

I'm furious at being held captive by such a spineless excuse of a human.

I break it all. I tear the books up until they're in tiny little pieces. I smash every last item, even the desk which I manage to hurl against the glass wall in a fit of rage.

It doesn't even scratch it slightly.

My temper gets worse, and I don't stop until every last thing is in pieces. Tiny, sharp pieces.

This tiny glass room is like my every nightmare come to life. In here I'm an object, a pretty and defenseless little thing to be admired and coveted by others. I never realized just how much autonomy and confidence Lips and Illi's training had given me. I had spent so long being protected by Ash and my family that I had started to think I was too weak to ever be able to take care of myself.

I know I can now.

If this wall of glass weren't here, I would've done something by now.

Chapter Twenty

The Collector's son doesn't come back into the room.

After I destroy everything, I sweep it all to one side of the enclosure with my foot as best as I can and then I sit down, curling my legs up underneath myself as much as I can without my skirt riding up. I'm sure I'll end up with tiny bits of porcelain cutting my legs open, but I don't care. I'm beyond caring about any of this anymore.

I pass out like that.

I wake up in the same sitting position I fell asleep, my ass aching and my bladder about to burst.

It almost kills me but I have to pee in the bucket.

It's either that or wet myself and I'd rather keep the bodily fluid as far away from me as possible, so I choose the lesser evil.

I'm going to burn this place to the fucking ground.

My mouth is dry as hell and my stomach rumbles but those are things I can ignore for now. Instead, I start looking for the sliding panels on the ground. If he slides the glass itself, there has to be a way to move it from the inside. These things always have fail-safes, some way that they design it to open just in case the builder or owner of it accidentally locks themselves inside the enclosure.

I'm a smart girl, if I can find the tracks I can figure out what it's going to take to get this thing open.

I don't know how long it takes but eventually I'm able to find the very end of the tracks, over by the back wall of the cage. It's minuscule, absolutely tiny, but there is a tiny gap.

Perfect.

I pick through the pile of debris until I find a tapered, stake-like piece of wood that was snapped off of the desk. It won't be easy but nothing in my life ever is.

I desperately want to strip out of my blazer, but I keep it on for the coverage. I'm going to stink by the time I get out of here but if that isn't motivation to get this bullshit over with, nothing is. It's too big at first but the more I push, the more the wood gets stripped away until eventually it slides in. The glass is too heavy to do much right now, but if I can jam more wood under there, maybe I can derail the rollers from the track and get the entire thing to come out.

It keeps me busy and hopeful. That's all I need right now.

I'm jamming a third spike into the gap when the door opens again and the man comes back, sweating and puffing like he's run the whole way. He holds the walkie-talkie to his face, his glasses slipping down his nose even further. "What do you think you're doing? Get up off of the floor! I don't have time for this sort of—"

He stops abruptly, his eyes widening as he looks around the room. I can't hear a thing, the ground isn't shaking, and there's nothing happening in my view point, so I just have to stare at the Collector's son and guess what the hell is going on.

"Get up now, girl! There's no way... how did he find it? He's had you microchipped, hasn't he? Filthy fucking Mounties, they're going to ruin everythi—"

His finger slips from the button and I can't hear anything else he's saying, but my heart sings in my chest.

Someone is here.

Someone found me.

I knew there was a good chance; I just had to stay alive in this stupid fucking glass cage for long enough that someone realized I was gone. This is a little sooner than I expected, but I'm not mad about it.

I need to get the hell away from the stinking blankets and the bucket of urine in the corner that I cannot think about without dry heaving.

His eyes widen again and then I feel it too.

The ground shakes.

He looks back up at me and presses a button on the walkie-talkie, his fingers trembling visibly. There's a soft *whoosh* sound on my side of the glass and then the clicking, crunching noise of the wood shards I just shoved in the gap breaking up. I scramble up onto my feet in time to see the most magical sight.

The glass starts to move as one, an opening appearing as if out of thin air.

My heart nearly bursts out of my chest with joy until I find a gun being pointed at my head with a hand that is still trembling enough to make him dangerous.

"Move. Out the door."

I huff and stalk forward, holding my hands out like he'll calm the hell down if it's obvious I'm not going to attempt to fight him.

It's a lie but, again, my appearance helps me to lull people into a false sense of security.

"Through to the elevator. Get in. Right, we're going to the third floor, don't even think about hitting the parking garage, I will put a bullet in your brain right now."

I roll my eyes because he wouldn't. I'm his hostage; I'm worthless to him dead. Well, I'm actually a ticking time bomb to him because either way he's dead. If he hands me over, loses me, kills me, no matter what he's fucking dead.

I'll kill him myself.

When the elevator door opens again, we find three men waiting in the lobby, all of them wearing suits. I get excited for half a second thinking they're the Crow's men, but then the Collector's son starts hurling insults and accusations at them.

"This is how you people do business, is it? Fucking pathetic! I was assured that I would have her without complication!

Amanda Donnelley said—"

One of the suits looks him up and down and cuts him off, "She assured you that she would get you the Wolf's Queen without complication. You've had twenty-two hours with her, surely you've gotten what you want out of her by now, Allan?"

I mark that man for death.

I imprint his face into my mind and memorize every little inch of it. I won't just have him taken out, I'll be making sure he gets the most brutal death I can arrange.

The Collector's son scoffs and stutters, "I—I don't want her for a night! Who pays that sort of money for a single night? This—you've robbed me!"

The suit shrugs, calm and collected even as the gunfire starts downstairs. "The Butcher spends his nights guarding her. She's coveted by the Crow and the Stag. She sits at the table of the Twelve and speaks for the Wolf. The last man who bought her, the man who truly owns her, is the Devil himself... what exactly were you expecting? She was never going to be here for long."

For the love of God.

This entire fucking kidnapping has been an exercise. Donnelley wanted to see how I would handle this sort of treatment, was probably hoping to break me with the memories of what happened with the Jackal and Diarmuid taking me.

This was all a test.

"I was expecting to get what I paid for! I was expecting to own her, to keep her in my collection. Fucking useless, how are

J Bree

we getting out of here?"

The suit shrugs and gestures to the other two men with him. "I have other business to attend to. Karlson and Mitchels will assist you in getting out of here. You better make it quick, the Crow is known for his temper when it comes to his queen."

Atticus.

Atticus is here once again to ride in and save me. I take a quick breath and then watch as the suit heads back down the lobby and disappears into a room, then the other two men step into the elevator with us.

They hit the button for the parking lot.

"What's the plan here? I don't want to lose my property, you know," the Collector's son says, the barrel of the gun pressing into the base of my skull.

Don't think about the trembling hands, Avery, for fuck's sake!

I can't help it though, because there's nothing more dangerous than a gun in nervous or inexperienced hands. It's why Illi had drilled safety and procedure into my head long before we actually started shooting, because he knew how badly I didn't want to touch the damn things.

"There's no way you can keep the girl. The plan is to survive, we can get you a replacement. Maybe you can choose one that has fewer... complications next time."

The Collector snarls and sputters, but it's too late to hear his argument.

The elevator door opens and all hell breaks loose.

"HOLD YOUR FIRE."

I'd recognize Luca's voice anywhere and the second it rings out, the bullets stop. There's suits everywhere, I can't tell who belongs to Donnelley and who belongs to the Crow, but everyone stops shooting the second I step out of the elevator, my hands still splayed and out from my sides a little.

"I'll give you the girl! Just let me leave here and she's yours!"

There's a haphazardly parked line of cars being used as cover, and as the smoke clears I see Luca weave through them, dressed completely in tactical gear. He has everything except the helmet on and a huge assault rifle slung over his chest like he's going to war.

He's still not my favorite person but fuck am I glad to see him right now.

"I'll clear a path for you but not until I have Avery."

The Collector's son scoffs and yells back, "Not fucking likely. You'll just kill me the second you have her. Give me a car and I'll let her out on the way."

There's an argument behind the line of cars and then Atticus steps out, a Kevlar vest over his chest and a gun in his hand, sure and steady. Luca huffs and tenses, like he's preparing to dive in front of his boss at the very first sign of more gunfire.

"I'll say this once. You have no idea of who you kidnapped. Hand her over or you'll find out."

I meet Atticus' eyes and I see the tells, the flex of his fingers and the shifting in his stance. Luca's hand hovers over the hand gun at his side, the rifle a distraction and one that's worked. They all are looking at it, and his hands being away from it entirely, and are seeing this as a white flag.

The moment my stance shifts, they know.

They know and they're trusting me to get it right, the maneuver I've practiced for months with Lips and Illi until my body works on autopilot.

Duck, turn, wrist, elbow, disarm.

Lips had said those five words to me until I was hearing them in my sleep. The moment the gun is pointed away from me, Luca and Atticus shoot the other two men, a headshot and one to the chest.

The Collector's son drops his gun and then I show him just how much of a pathetic little rich bitch I am not, because there isn't anything quite as satisfying as breaking the asshole's nose with my knee as he attempts to swoop down for the gun. I still desperately wish that I wasn't wearing the skirt, but desperate times call for desperate measures and Lips always did say my thighs were a concealed weapon.

The moment he rears back, Atticus shoots him in the chest.

There's more bullets flying around us and Atticus rushes at me, crowding me against the wall and using his body as a shield.

"Are you hurt? There's blood on your skirt; where are you bleeding from, Avery?"

I glance down and then back up to meet his eyes. "It's not mine. I'm fucking furious, but I'm fine. I'd murder someone for a glass of water and a hamburger."

He huffs, grunting as a couple of bullets get a little too close for comfort and ducking his head further into mine until I'm completely surrounded by him. There's a moment of silence, the gunfire ceasing around us and then the Crow's men start calling out, "Clear!"

Over and over again until Atticus finally straightens up. It's like a military operation now, the months since they'd taken out the Jackal and his men had obviously involved a lot more training.

"How did you find me?"

Atticus takes a step away from me, pulling at the straps and fastenings of his vest. "I've had him tailed for months; I knew where this place was. The moment I realized Amanda had gotten into my phone I came here."

He pulls the Kevlar over my head and when I try to argue, he snarls at me, "You'll fucking wear it until I get you home safe. All the way home, all the way into your house with the door closed."

I nod along, feeling happy enough at him being alive and safe that I let him fuss over me for a minute. He didn't just charge in, swing me over his shoulder, and ride off to find a tower to hide me in.

He trusted me to do what I'd been trained to do.

Luca walks over to us slowly, approaching as if he's worried I'll take a swing at him.

Or stab him.

If I were armed, I might.

"We got everyone; the place is clear. I'm glad you're okay, Avery. You had us worried for a second there."

I take a deep breath but my words still come out too harsh. "Did your men take out the suit on the third floor? No? Then you didn't get everyone and that man needed a very messy death."

Luca nods curtly and glances at Atticus before stepping away, speaking into an earpiece while they track down the other guy. I'm not stupid, I know he could've gone to a different floor, but I can feel it in my gut that he's slipped through our fingers somehow.

I'll find him.

Finding assholes like that is kind of my specialty.

"It's not Luca's fault, you know. Jack's death is on me for not taking the Bear out sooner. I shouldn't have held onto the sanctity of the favors so hard. We all knew he was going to be a problem. It was my call and I made the wrong one."

I blink rapidly and shrug. "I did too. I should have listened to my gut and sent Illi after him the moment we realized we needed three seats. Jack's death is mine."

Atticus frowns at me and takes my chin in his hand. "No, I'm not going to let you carry that weight, Avery. It's too fucking much, even for someone as strong as you."

I blink away my tears and push myself up into his chest, pressing our lips together for a second. He pulls away and looks me over one last time, just to be sure I'm not hurt. Then he tucks me back up under his arm, holding me close to him as we make our way over to the car.

The gunshot isn't loud.

It's barely a pop sound but the damage is incredible. I've seen dozens of bullet wounds thanks to my time with Lips, but there's still something very different about seeing the exit wound tear your life-long love's chest apart.

Atticus drops to the ground.

I go down with him, untouched but fucking destroyed.

Luca starts screaming out orders and the Collector's son is dead a second later but, once again, we're too late.

"Avery, Avery move. I need to get pressure on this."

"It's—you can't—it's too late," I gasp out, and Luca firmly shoves me aside.

"You're in shock, step away. It's bad but he's not dead yet. Call for an airlift!" He screams the last part and I blink at him because I don't know what the hell he means, but then there's people running around us everywhere.

There's a hole the size of my fist in his chest.

There's no surviving that.

"Avery, shut your fucking mouth. His heart is still beating and until it stops, you can keep that shit to yourself. He never gave up on you, don't you fucking dare give up on him."

A sob rips out of my throat and I watch in horror as Luca and two other men pack Atticus' chest with whatever they can to staunch the blood loss. There's no stopping it, only slowing it down a little. His eyes are still open, rolling back in his head as his body spasms. I can't do this.

I can't do this at all.

I crawl over to his head, careful not to get in anyone else's way because even as spaced out as my brain is, I know that's important. I lift my hands up to cup his cheeks but they're covered in blood, tiny shards of glass sticking out of them.

I glance down and, yes, I did just crawl over glass to get to him.

I feel nothing.

I put my hands back down, because I don't want to cover his face with my blood and instead, I lower my forehead to his. I can hear the tiniest rattling wheeze of his breath and there's nothing I can give him right now, nothing but me being here with him until the very end.

The way he's always been with me.

"I love you. I've loved you since I was nine years old and you punched out one of the Davids boys in the face for lifting up my skirt at that stupid gala. I've loved you through middle school and high school. I waited for you to notice me and love me back. I've loved you for as long as I've been breathing and I will love you long after I stop."

The Ruthless

Chapter Twenty-One

Atticus

Five Years Ago

I kill the next buyer but not before he manages to stab me and attempt to gut me. He gets a little too close for comfort, the knife definitely hitting some very important organs, and blood is pouring out of me at an alarming rate.

He'd approached Senior after news had spread about yet another of his deals falling through thanks to the buyer disappearing from the map. The rumors are that Beaumont himself is killing them off once he's got the money from the sale, but anyone who believes that of the billionaire serial killer is too dense to be a concern.

No, this buyer enjoyed a challenge, and being the first person to actually survive the exchange and take Avery home with them is a challenge he was willing to die for.

And die he does.

He was faster than I was expecting with his own knife, sinking it deep in my gut and dragging it a good three inches before my own knife slices through his neck and rips his carotid in half.

It's a very quick and bloody way to go, I'm merciful like that.

I get out of the back alleyway I called the buyer to meet me in, lurching and stumbling all over the place, dry heaving as my body goes into shock. I have a very small amount of time to get out of here before my limbs and unnecessary organs begin to shut down.

I bleed everywhere.

There'll be DNA to clean up for days. I'm not usually this sloppy, more than aware of how easy it is to blackmail and manipulate people with the right evidence, but my only focus right now is getting to my car. I need to get the hell out of here before one of the Jackal's men spots me and takes me out. It's no secret he has a bounty on my head and a long list of men desperate enough to do the job. The Butcher has proved there is a chance of survival if you kill a member, it's just not great odds.

That glimmer of hope does crazy things though.

Part of his business plan is to keep his people poor, addicted, and miserable so they follow his every command, begging and hopeful that he'll throw them some scraps like some archaic overlord. The Bay is a desolate place but only the most desperate wear the Jackal's mark.

There's the scrape of boots on the sidewalk and I clench my

teeth as I stumble a little faster, my own feet dragging along like two lumps of concrete at the end of my legs. I can't feel anything from the knee down.

My hands are numb too.

There's a voice calling out to me, but all of my focus is on my Bentley and closing the gap to it. Ten feet, nine, eight—I'm getting there. The closest hospital is the worst in the country, but it'll have to do, because the three minute drive there might already be too much for my current state, but I have no choice here.

Get there or die.

"What the hell did you do now, Crawford? Fucking hell, stop moving before you bleed out all over the fucking sidewalk."

I stop and turn to find Luca stalking over to me, still wearing the Mounty standard uniform of dirty jeans, a tight tee, and a leather jacket.

"You can't be seen with me."

He scoffs and ducks under my arm, pressing his own hand to the wound like he's trying to hold my guts in single-handedly.

Well.

I guess he is.

He growls at me, frustration radiating through every line of him. "Yeah and none of it means a fucking thing if you're dead, boss."

I shrug because I just don't fucking care anymore. The moments that I let myself feel despair and self-loathing are rare, but the blood loss means I'm not coherent enough to stop it. "Dying for her has always been the plan. Who am I to complain about having my greatest wish fulfilled?"

He groans at me and shoves me into the passenger seat of my car, racing around to go in the driver's seat and then we're flying down the backstreets and back onto the highway, "Oh yeah? And who's taking care of her when you're gone? Who's going to go toe-to-toe with her fucking psychotic father if you're not around?"

I hit the recline on the seat to lessen the pressure on my wound and press a hand back over the mess of my stomach, blood smearing over every part of the car I'm touching. "You do. You'll take care of her for me."

He looks over to me in the darkness of the car and gives me a curt nod. "To the end."

The Ruthless

Chapter Twenty-Two

"*You own my soul, Atticus Crawford. I love you. I love you.*"

I say those three words, over and over again, even after they finally get him out of the building and airlifted away in the helicopter. Even after they give me a headset of my own because I refuse to leave his side.

Even after they take him into the operating room and I know it's the last I'll ever see of him, in my mind I say it because somewhere in the back of my mind I'm sure he can hear it.

He'll die knowing I love him the same now as I always have.

I sit, covered in blood, in the waiting room staring at the wall blankly. I don't know how long I've been there or anything about what's happening around me. When I'd climbed into the helicopter with Atticus, Luca had sent a couple of men with us, so I assume they're around somewhere keeping an eye on me but I have no real clue of the details.

I don't want to know about them.

I don't want to exist right now, right up until I hear his voice call out from down the hospital corridor.

"Queenie."

I crumple to the dirty hospital floor, slipping out of my chair and just fucking sobbing like a child. The glass in my hands digs even further into my skin, but the sting barely registers. I just fall into a heap because my soul just ripped into two. Aodhan might hold half of it tightly in his hands, but Atticus is about to leave this Earth with the other half.

I'm bereft without him.

"I've got you, baby. I'm never letting go, we'll stay right fucking here until you're ready," Aodhan says, his voice low and calm as he pulls me into his arms. I sob until there's nothing left of me.

When he gets an eyeful of my hands, Aodhan flags down a nurse and we're led into the procedure room to have the glass removed. Aodhan murmurs kind and calming things into my ear, but I barely feel the digging of the tools over the pain in my chest. The shards are tiny enough that the nurse only had to glue the wounds shut, giving me a list of things I shouldn't do that I don't even bother to listen to.

Aodhan takes the pamphlet from her and tucks it into his pocket, leading me back out to the waiting lounge and getting me settled back into one of the chairs. I've spent way too much time in these fucking chairs over the last few years.

"My phone is gone."

Aodhan nods and drapes his arms around me. "I know,

baby. Odie went into labor and when you didn't answer his calls and texts, Illi sent me around to your place. I found about a hundred of the Crow's men there and I figured out what the fuck happened to you from there. He already had you back by then… we already knew he'd been shot. I came right over."

I nod and sniff a little, my eyes stinging but I have no tears left in me now. "Donnelley lured me out. She hijacked Atticus' number and asked to meet then sold me off to one of the men she hired to watch me."

Aodhan's arm tightens around my shoulder and I shake my head. "I was only there for a day before Atticus came. The guy was a fucking lunatic, but I'm fine. I got a little too lucky there and Atticus has paid the price."

Aodhan scowls and shakes his head at me, shifting and pulling his phone out as it buzzes. He stares at the screen for a second and then moves the screen so I can read the message from Illi.

We're at the same hospital. Maternity wing. Tell the kid I'll deal with everything once we're out. Odie is doing good. Updates soon.

We're all here together. One life entering the world while another leaves it. There's a beauty to the cycles of life that I'd really love to tear up and burn to the ground, because I cannot do this.

"Breathe, Queenie. Just breathe it out, no use panicking about shit until we know more. He's in with surgeons; they know their shit. Just take a deep breath. Fuck, lemme go grab you some water."

They work on Atticus for eight hours.

I don't move from my seat. Aodhan makes phone calls to cover shit with his family and mine, then he arranges food for us both and spends an hour convincing me to eat mine. He watches everyone who walks past us like a hawk, ready to take someone out without hesitation if they so much as look sideways at me.

When a doctor finally comes out to see us, he informs me that I'm listed as Atticus' emergency contact and that I can go back to see him, though I'll have to go alone.

It takes me a second to understand that he's saying Atticus is still breathing.

My joy lasts half a second.

I follow the doctor through the corridors as he updates me, the situation getting worse and worse the more he speaks. "He's lost a lot of blood, and there has been a lot of damage done internally. I need to warn you that we've had to leave his chest cavity open for now, we'll see how he does over the next few days before we make any more decisions. Right now, we're focusing on getting him through the night."

He leaves me at the door of the ICU room, the machines all beeping at different pitches and frequencies in a nightmare of sounds.

Atticus looks like a corpse.

I stay with him for an hour, holding his hand and stroking back the front of his hair where he leaves a little of the length.

He looks peaceful, calm, and completely gone.

There's no real way of doing it, but I try to make my peace. I try to say all of the things I need to say to him in this moment and hope that he can hear me. I beg him to stay. I beg him to never leave me, to stay and come home to me so we can work this out.

Then I kiss him as best I can with all of the tubes breathing for him.

I walk back out to Aodhan who looks relieved the second he spots me, drawing me into his arms and kissing the top of my head gently, like he has to treat me with kid gloves right now. I have no tears left to cry, my entire body hollowed out until I'm nothing but a shell.

"Illi called. The baby is here. We don't have to go down if—"

"No. No, we absolutely do have to go down. This is a huge moment for him, he's family. He, Odie, and the baby are family."

The maternity ward is on the other side of the hospital and we have to ask for directions twice before we find it. Aodhan sends Illi a message from the waiting room, and I try not to look at all of the posters of happy, smiling couples holding their bundles of joy. I'm too raw for that.

After a minute, Illi steps out of one of the rooms and I force myself to meet his eyes.

This is the happiest day of his life.

I won't ruin it, no matter that it's the worst day of mine.

After everything he's done for me, I cannot ruin this too.

"It's a boy. Odie wants to call him Johnny… I think I'm going to let her."

I hold my arms open and he crushes me to his chest. "Why do you smell like blood? What the fuck—"

"It doesn't matter. Tomorrow. We can talk about it tomorrow. Today is for Johnny and Odie. How is she? I know she had concerns."

He beams at me, the type of smile I didn't even know his face was capable of making. "She did fucking amazing. I almost killed three nurses but she was a fucking pro. He's fucking beautiful, looks just like his mama."

My eyes fill with tears, but I guess that's normal around this sort of news. "Illi, I'm so happy for you both. Congratulations, I cannot wait to meet him. I need to go home and clean up; I have a gift waiting there for you all already."

Aodhan reaches around me to shake Illi's hand, jerking in shock when Illi crushes him in a hug too. It's that back slapping, brotherhood sort of hug but Aodhan still looks stunned that it's happening.

I wish I could enjoy the look a little more.

"Go back to your family, Illi. We'll be back in the morning to meet your son, I promise. I need to clean up and be presentable," I say, my voice still strong but I'm not sure how much longer I can hold out.

Illi looks me over again and then nods slowly. "Okay.

Tomorrow. I'll give you until tomorrow, Queenie."

It'll be better tomorrow.

It has to be.

"You need a shower and a bed, you look like something out of the Walking Dead," Aodhan murmurs as we take the elevator back down to the exit.

I want to make a joke about it but instead I shrug and thread my fingers through his, yawning until my jaw pops. "I would commit cold-blooded murder for a shower right now. And a new set of clothes, I'm burning this entire outfit."

Aodhan chuckles and pulls a lighter out of his pocket. "I can help with that."

I roll my eyes and then narrow them at him. "I didn't know you smoke."

"I don't. It's for more... nefarious things. You never know when you need a distraction."

I shake my head at him, leaning on him and taking some of his strength. Jesus fucking Christ, he lost his cousin and best friend days ago. The grieving process for him will have barely started and already I'm having to ask things of him, to lean on him to get me through this.

I feel like a burden to him.

We step outside of the hospital and Luca is there waiting, a cigarette hanging out of his mouth which is very unusual for him.

Aodhan stiffens a little but he doesn't lunge at him and choke him out, so it's not as bad as it could be.

I still don't want to look at him, even after the hurried conversation with Atticus before—

Before.

"I need you both to come back to the Crow's mansion."

I flinch back and Aodhan snaps, "Absolutely not. What the fuck is wrong with you? I'll put you in the ground right the fuck now, don't push me."

Luca puts the cigarette out on the ground, stepping on it and turning toward us both. He looks like he's aged twenty years in the last week and I know exactly what that feels like. "There's been an emergency Twelve meeting called. I've arranged for it to be at the Crow's residence because it's the most secure and your safety is still at risk. You need to attend, both of you."

Aodhan takes a step toward him and when Luca widens his stance like he's ready to have this brawl right here on the hospital steps, I have to stand in-between them. "Luca, I can't do it tonight. I can't be who they need me to be tonight. Postpone it or something."

Luca glances over to me and the sorrow pouring out of him is suffocating. "Avery. Atticus left it all to you. Everything, his entire empire. If he doesn't pull through this then every single thing that he's worked so fucking hard for… it's all yours. If you don't come to the meeting now and stand your ground, who knows what will happen. This could spiral out of control faster than you can imagine and then there'll be a whole new war to face. Do you want that for us all?"

I absolutely do not want that for any of us, not for the man I'm in love with up there in the ICU or the new family of three in the maternity wing who are living through the greatest night of their lives right now. Not for Lips who's out there somewhere in a tour bus full of guys that she's madly in love with and will throw herself into hell for without a second thought.

I can't let my own personal problems affect the overall good.

Aodhan looks down at me and sees the decision in my eyes, already made for us all and nods. "Fine. We'll head over there. Do you have enough security here to cover Crawford for the night?"

Luca nods at him like that's a stupid question and reaches into his pocket, pulling out my phone. "I found this in your Rolls Royce, it must've been left behind there. Probably because they didn't want us tracking you that way. It's run out of battery, but at least it survived your ordeal."

I take it and slip it back into my pocket, the weight of it familiar and a small comfort. Aodhan waits for a second and then walks me over to the Impala, helping me in and buckling the seatbelt around me while he clucks about my torn-up hands.

I've still barely even noticed they're injured. I'm sure they'll sting like a bitch tomorrow.

The drive over to Atticus' mansion is silent, neither of us

happy about where we're headed but for very different reasons. Aodhan hates Atticus and fucking loathes Luca so going to that place will be the last thing he wants to do. I, however, need to stay strong to get through this and sitting in that house, surrounded by all of the Crow's people and things, it'll be too much for me. It'll all make me want to sit and wallow in him.

Wallow in the pain and fear.

The men at the gate let us straight through with barely a glance inside the car, and we're directed by the groundsmen on where to park. Aodhan grimaces and mumbles unhappily about the entire process but follows me up into the house without complaint.

I take the world's quickest shower in one of the downstairs guest rooms.

Okay, it's five minutes but considering how freaking disgusting I feel, it's life-changing. Utterly freaking life-changing. I wash my hair twice in that time and scrub every inch of myself with a loofa. Aodhan offers to come in and scrub my back for me, but I feel far too disgusting for that. I know he's offering to help me rush through this and taking his eyes off of me right now is proving to be very difficult, but the moment I peel the clothing away from me, the stench of my sweat truly hits me and I gag.

I can't believe Aodhan has insisted on being so close to me while I've freaking reeked.

Aodhan rolls his eyes at my very obvious panic from the

doorway, his arms crossed over his chest and a frown over his face. "Don't be fucking stupid, Queenie, like I'd ever give a fuck about that shit."

I duck back into my room here to choose clothing and go with a white dress with a thigh slit so high I can wear a set of thigh holsters underneath it without any worries of being able to access them. It has a long sleeve and a high neckline, so once I do a full face of makeup and slick my straightened hair back, the entire look is regal and deadly.

The exact combination I'm going for here.

Aodhan walks me in, obviously very aware that the Butcher isn't here to watch my back and shed blood for me. I'm not worried. I have the knives and more than enough of the Crow's men to protect me.

When we take our seats, Luca stands directly behind my seat. Every one of the members sees it and knows exactly what it means.

Jackson walks in looking subdued and gives me a very open and respectful nod of greeting, sitting beside Aodhan without a word. All of the other seats fill up quickly but with five missing members it looks very empty at the table.

Everyone looks uncomfortable as hell.

I have no real clue on how to start so I go with polite for now, taking a leaf out of Atticus' book. "Good evening. Thank you for coming on such short notice."

The Viper scoffs, looking a little bit drunk and maybe high. "Like we had a fucking choice. Four suits show up to my fight and say I have to leave to come up here: it's fucking bullshit. So the Crow is half dead, who fucking cares? Call me when he's cold and then maybe I'll give a shit."

I turn to him and eye him slowly, choosing all of the best places to stab him if it comes down to that.

I'd really like it to come down to that.

"I just wanted to make a few things clear to you all—"

He interrupts me, his words slurring a little. "You mean the part where your little fucking 'family' is killing off members of the Twelve faster than we can replace them? How long until you come after us too, huh? Fuck, I thought the Crow was safe since he was bending you over but you really are just a cold-hearted piece of pussy, aren't you?"

I'm done.

I'm done with this conversation and with the complete and utter bullshit that is the Twelve.

Faster than any of them imagine, I'm sure, I unsheathe my knife from the thigh holster and impale it through the Viper's hand and into the table below.

He lets out a roar, and Luca inserts himself between the two of us before the Viper can take a swing at me.

"Lips told me all about how you lost your fingers. I've seen them, you know? The Butcher has them pickled in a jar down in his workshop. I recognized the stupid fucking knuckle tats straight away. Where I'm going with this is that you'd think a man like you would learn your lesson about who not to fuck with, but… you really haven't learned, have you? There isn't an opening for power here, no gaps to be filled or businesses to take over. There's just the Wolf of Mounts Bay and the Family who back her. The Crow was voted in and while he's indisposed, he's named me to speak for him."

I look around the room and not a word is spoken between them. Only Jackson and Aodhan will meet my eyes, the rest are looking around like they're a little too aware that this might be it for them. That I've lost all ability to play by their rules and if they don't toe the line, I'll destroy them.

Slowly and with great pleasure.

I lean around Luca to grab the handle of the knife and yank it out, the Viper grunting and clutching his hand to his chest as blood drips freaking everywhere.

"You are either a member of the Twelve who respects the rules, minds their own business, and lives a happy life… or you're dead. No one is attempting to take your cage fights away. I don't give a shit about the Ox's protection racket or the Boar's imports. The parties are a great night out for us, and the Tiger is helpful when things get messy around here. We're not trying to change what you're all doing, we're just letting you know that everything else going on in the Bay? It belongs to us. I don't want a skin market so there won't be one. End of discussion.

You want to buy, go live somewhere else. I'm not asking for a lot from you people, this is all very basic shit."

The Boar looks up at me and says, "Are we done here? Some of us have real work to do and I have no fucking interest in this little lecture. You already know where I stand when it comes to the Wolf."

Huh.

I don't like him.

I've never liked the Boar because he stood by and watched his niece live through absolute fucking hell for years, all while patting himself on the back for looking out for her.

Piece of shit.

"Sure. Get the fuck out of my house, the lot of you, and don't start anything you can't see through to the end. We'll see you all at the next stage of the Game."

They all stand up and file out. The Tiger hangs back for a second and looks as though he's going to vomit but approaches me anyway.

"If, ah, if the Crow doesn't pull through, you need to call me. I've done all of his estate planning, and there's a very sizable estate to pass along to you. He was very clear to me about what was going to be happening and where it's all going."

I nod and wave him on because now isn't at all the time for that discussion.

I'm not thinking about it until I absolutely have to.

The Ruthless

Chapter Twenty-Three

Atticus's mansion had always been a quiet place, all of the men and women who worked here kept to themselves, but it had never been this morbid before.

Aodhan hates it. "Honestly, Queenie, I'd rather have my toenails pulled out with a set of pliers than stay here. What the fuck are we going to do, sleep in his bed? I would've been fine fucking you where he sleeps a few days ago but after he took a bullet to save you, I feel like an asshole even bringing it up."

I roll my eyes at him, still hollowed out at the thought of the gaping hole in Atticus' chest. "I have my own bed here, obviously. You can sleep in there with me tonight, and in the morning we can figure out how much of this empire I can run from my house and how much requires me to be here."

He nods, a little distracted, and tucks me under his arm as we walk. I direct him the entire way down the hall until we tuck ourselves into the lavish room that Atticus had put aside for me. I know for sure it isn't just a guest room because the soaps, hair products, and skin care brands are all exactly what I use at home. The sheets are the same as mine, all of the colors are what I would pick out for myself, and there's no less than eight pillows on the bed which I'm sure isn't a standard number but is my own preference.

"So do all super fucking rich people like the same shit or did you do the decorating in here? Jesus. It even has the fucking bed-couch thing like yours."

I giggle at his description of the chaise longue as I strip off my blazer, grabbing my phone out from my pocket. There's a couple of missed calls from Lips, but I need a shower and a few hours in Aodhan's arms before I let the real world touch me again.

I don't think I can handle Lips comforting me about Atticus right now. I'll break wide open and I don't have the time for that sort of breakdown; I need a clear head to do what's right for him and his people.

"A chaise longue is vital to any well-designed bedroom. Where else will Lips sit and hate every minute of helping me plan out my wardrobe for the season? Or where else would Harley have sat and moped to me that he wants to fuck the new scholarship Mounty girl, but she has a knife and knows how to use it? I have a hundred more examples for you."

He tugs his shirt over his head and stalks over to the offending piece of furniture, dropping down onto it and getting comfortable. "It could work as a sex bench. Climb up and sit that pretty pussy on me, Queenie."

I huff at him and saunter into the bathroom, swinging my hips as I go and smirking at his answering groan. "I need to freshen up first. Give me a minute."

He doesn't say a word about it, mostly because he's aware of the five minute shower I took when we first left the hospital and there's no way that will be enough for me to relax now and enjoy being with him. My hands sting when the water hits them and I'm sure I'm ruining the glue, but my OCD wins out for now. I'll have to fix them later.

I also need five minutes to process the guilt and loathing at myself for being here in Atticus' house, fucking my *other* lover, while he's in a hospital dying.

Atticus has always, always done things for the greater good.

Being here and taking over his business for him while he's out of the picture is, without a doubt, the greater good, but the guilt may still eat me alive.

"Stop fucking thinking about it. There's nothing we can do for him up at that hospital and you left enough men up there guarding him to take out a fucking president if they have to. We're here because he would want you here."

He's right, I know he's right, but I still feel the crushing weight of the evening bearing down on me. "I always thought we'd figure our problems out and find our way back to each other. I... I had just decided to talk to him properly about making this work. About having you both and feeling whole again and then

I was taken. He gave me his vest, Aodhan. If he hadn't, if he had've just waited—"

Aodhan cuts me off with a savage snarl, "If he hadn't, it would be you in that fucking hospital bed and I don't feel an ounce of guilt saying I'm glad it's him and not you. Crawford is glad it's him and not you, I can say that without even thinking about it. He's a fucking asshole of a man, but he's been nothing but consistent when it comes to you. Whatever the cost, he was going to get you home safe. Why the hell do you think I'm okay sharing you with him? I couldn't give a fuck about history or any of that shit, I can share with him because I want you happy, healthy, and whole. He was a fucking big part of that."

I take a deep breath, the tears streaming out of me and spilling all over the freaking place but I can't acknowledge them. I need to stop. I need to pull myself together and be the woman in charge.

Luca had called me the Queen Crow, but I feel like a freaking imposter right now.

"Baby, stop. Stop crying, we're going to go to bed. We're going to be done with this fucked night and we're going to get back up tomorrow swinging. No one touches the Family and lives."

I choke on a sob, stepping out of the shower and into the towel he's holding out to me. He wraps me up and bundles me into his arms.

"He's not family, he said so himself."

Aodhan shakes his head. "He's got my vote. Lips' and Harley's, yours. Illi and Odie will vote for him after they hear the story... fuck, Illi might vote for him just for what he did to the Bear. Six to two means he's in."

I clear my throat. "That makes it a six-all tie. There's still Jackson, Viola, and... two of Lips' siblings. I think Jackson would vote for him though."

He nods slowly, not asking any questions. "Put the call out. Get the official vote and get him in. No more tip-toeing around this shit. If your brother has issues, he can come talk to me about them."

As I follow him back out into the bedroom to get dressed, I snort at him, the most un-Avery sound he's probably ever heard, but really? "You're going to face off with Ash over Atticus? I've officially heard it all."

He shakes his head at me like I'm freaking dense. "You're mine. I'll face off with Ash for you and for any reason you might have. He's your brother and I respect that but you're mine and we make our decisions about how our life goes, not him."

I've never heard anything sexier or more terrifying in my life.

Then the lights go out, the entire room plunges into darkness.

"Fuck. Get your ass over here, Queenie," Aodhan says, bending back down to rummage through his clothing for his gun. I use the light on my phone to get back around the bed without bumping into the furniture.

I message Luca quickly.

What's going on?

Once he has his gun, Aodhan shoves his legs back into his jeans and buttons them back up, foregoing a shirt but at least he's not going to be facing… whatever this is in his boxers.

"Grab some pants and your gun. Fuck, where's your vest? Put that on too."

I quickly pull on yoga pants and the Kevlar, strapping my knife onto my thigh and grabbing my gun. I take a deep breath and quickly look it over, exactly the way Illi taught me. The safety is on, and I position my finger ready to take it off the moment I need to.

Aodhan watches me closely and when I meet his eyes, he says, "You good? I'll take point and you can just watch our backs until we find Veltori."

It takes me a second to remember that he means Luca, my brain still sluggish after the trauma of the last few days, and I nod. My phone buzzes in my hand again, but after a glance I ignore it. I can call Lips back the moment we know what the hell is going on here.

I walk with Aodhan, shining the light to lead us both and we pause at the door, just long enough for him to listen out but there's nothing out there, no sound to tell us a thing of what's happening.

My phone buzzes again and this time it's Luca.

Donnelley has sent men for you. Stay where you are, we're handling it.

Jesus.

I turn the phone for Aodhan to see it right as the door rips open and someone grabs his arm, pulling him away from me even as he opens fire.

I'm going to lose them both.

Aodhan is jerked away from me and out of the room, but with the spotlight on my phone I can see them well enough to shoot. I don't recognize them and I pray Luca didn't send them up here to come retrieve us.

Aodhan takes two out and I take care of the other three, simple and effective shots to the chest. I shine the light down onto each of them and make sure there's blood coming out of the bullet holes, that they're not wearing bulletproof vests.

There's the sound of more gunfire, and I want to freaking scream.

"We're sitting fucking ducks up here, Queenie. Can you get us to the tunnel? The one you use to sneak out?" Aodhan breathes the words to me, barely loud enough for me to hear over the pounding of my heart.

I nod because at this point I could do it in my sleep. Two flights of stairs, a long hallway, and the dining room to go through though, so a lot of places to be caught in.

Aodhan starts to move, turning when I tap him on the shoulder as we slowly, quietly, and carefully make our way downstairs. We make it all the way down to the ground floor before we run into more suits, and this time I don't hesitate to start shooting.

Aodhan takes four of them out before he throws himself at a fifth, his knife in his hand as he grapples with the man. He's a natural brawler and kills the man with ease. Then five more suits come around the corner and I open fire, taking down four of them while Aodhan takes the fifth on at hand-to-hand.

I'm out of bullets, the gun completely useless to me now, but I have the holster with knives still strapped to me, if anyone gets that close.

"Get out, Avery. Go, I'll meet you there."

He doesn't say where exactly, just in case, but I wait until I see him get the upper hand before I scramble away from them both. There's no way I'm going to leave him behind but I need to find more guns for us both to go the rest of the way, and one of the guys I just took out would have to have been armed.

I step into the dining room and come to an abrupt halt.

The panel to the tunnel is already wide open, and a living skeleton is climbing through the hidden doorway.

Bing.

He looks up at me and his eyes flare with recognition, his body turning toward me and every little bit of his focus is now pointed in my direction.

His hair is overgrown and he's more bones than body, but the feral look in his eye is an echo of the manic energy Joey used to give off, and I know there's no way I can underestimate him.

Think, Avery, think!

There's no time to think though, because he rushes at me, swinging his fists with no sort of coordination. He looks like a caveman dragging his knuckles along the ground, and I watch in horror for a second too long, trapped by the shock of seeing him like this.

I get my hand around the handle of my knife a second too late, and his hands wrap around my throat at the same time as my knife sinks into his gut.

His eyes widen and a surprised look takes over his features. He fucking stinks up this close and his fingers are brittle and boney around my neck. When his lip curls, I slide the knife out and plunge it in again, praying I'm hitting organs inside him that will kill him quickly.

His fingers loosen a little more, slipping on my neck until he almost lets go. I give the knife one last yank and then I feel something more than blood come out of his stomach and land on my feet.

He collapses.

I vomit.

When I get the heaving to stop, I shake my foot off without looking and then I step around Bing's prone form until I can reach his neck. I'm not going to leave any chance of survival for him.

I slit his throat, dragging the knife as deeply as I can and then watching the blood pour out of him all over the ground and myself.

It's done.

I stand there and pray it's all over when the lights abruptly come back on, the front entrance lighting up completely. I blink a little and the front door slides open slowly, a tall, dark and very familiar figure stalking through the doorway.

A sob of relief rips through my throat.

The knife falls from my hand as Ash stares at me, his eyes like dark, bottomless voids. My heart feels as though it's going to burst out of my chest.

He's home.

I'm safe.

I take a step forward, my feet slipping a little in the blood, but he doesn't react. He doesn't come forward to tug me into his arms or crush me to his chest like he usually does when I'm freaking the hell out. He doesn't yell and run at me; there's no arguing over what's happened.

There's nothing on his face at all.

Until Aodhan steps around the corner and the quiet, deadly, killing rage visibly fills him. The type that doesn't mean a beating, it means death.

"*You.*"

The Ruthless

Also by J Bree

The Mounts Bay Saga

The Butcher Duet
The Butcher of the Bay: Part I
The Butcher of the Bay: Part II

Hannaford Prep
Just Drop Out: Hannaford Prep Year One
Make Your Move: Hannaford Prep Year Two
Play the Game: Hannaford Prep Year Three
To the End: Hannaford Prep Year Four

The Queen Crow Trilogy
All Hail
The Ruthless
Queen Crow

Standalone Novels
Angel Unseen: An Unseen MC Novel

About J Bree

J Bree is a dreamer, writer, mother, farmer, and cat-wrangler. The order of priorities changes daily.

She lives on a small farm in a tiny rural town in Australia that no one has ever heard of. She spends her days dreaming about all of her book boyfriends, listening to her partner moan about how the wine grapes are growing, and being a snack bitch to her two kids.

For updates about upcoming releases, please visit her website at http://www.jbreeauthor.com, and sign up for the newsletter or join her group on Facebook at #mountygirlforlife: A J Bree Reading Group

Made in the USA
Las Vegas, NV
15 January 2024

84443817R00184